Bigfoot and the Tripwire

Footprints of a Legend

Russell Victor Acord

Dedication

I want to thank my mother; Sandra, for always being there throughout my life. Not once have you ever been unfair or spoken despairingly towards another person. I think we can all learn from those characteristics and follow your example of that unconditional love for family and friends. Your unwavering strength and high moral standards was the compass where our family found our direction. As a mother of seven children and a supportive wife to Victor for over fifty years; I dedicate this book to you Mom.

Special Thanks

There will always be that personal story around an author who will spend endless hours writing a novel and the sacrifices that are made. It is all about the passion from within and the deep desire to share our creativity. I appreciate the encouragement by all my family members and my readers to finish this second story and put it out there on the shelves. I want to thank my wife Kelly and my wonderful daughter Adrienne; who stuck with me as I took our family vacation time away from them. Without your help and understanding this second book would not have naturally flowed onto the following pages. With heartfelt love and appreciation; I thank you, and I love you. Now let's go back to Montana and get that third book finished!

Bigfoot and the Tripwire

A Novel By

Russell Victor Acord

Acknowledgment of Artwork

I need to share that I couldn't have made the connection of the face I saw in my mind's eye without the masterful art of Pam McKee. Not only representing the cover of this book and its illustrations, she is also the artist for my Footprints of a Legend novel. Pam grew up as my childhood friend and neighbor in Florence Montana, not far from Kootenai Mountain and the backdrop of this entire story. Pam's artwork has given our readers a face to put with the mystical creatures within the pages of this novel. Pam also has gone on to publish her own books and is available to create artwork for other authors and business owners.

Thank You Pamela!

gravamengallery.net

Forward

The time-line of this book is based from 1970 to 2007. The 70's were a busy time when the Vietnam War was captivating the headlines and we had less access to the media at our fingertips. The references to Vietnam are written out of deep respect for the soldiers who took the oath years before my own military service. It is my intent to honor those who served during this time period and under no circumstances is offense intended. I want to thank Bill Carroll, my Vietnam Veteran friend from Idaho. The Bitterroot Mountains of Montana will call all walks of life into their majestic beauty; some for all the wrong reasons, and others a life that is built on purity and peace. These worlds often cross paths which do not always mix well. If you relate to the following pages and the adventure that you are about to embark on; please share your experience with your friends and let them know where to find this novel. I am self-published and my success is largely decided through you; the reader, by word of mouth. Thank you for your interest in Bigfoot and the Tripwire; the prequel of my 'Footprints of a Legend' series. I hope you enjoy this novel as much as I have enjoyed writing it. And for the record; I couldn't have done this without the candid editing and discussion of Melissa Reijm; thank you, and be on the lookout for book number three.

Chapter Index

The Diary of LT John Stone
Bitterroot Series

My name is Lieutenant John Stone; in keeping count of the winters that have passed I guess that the year is 2006 or 2007. The story I'm about to share with you is an incredible series of events that need to be remembered. I know my days on this green earth are limited and what I have experienced cannot die with me. Reading back over the following pages I have a hard time believing it myself; but when I'm gone there will be no one to share my story or have any idea of what really exists up here in the high country. My diary is all I have, if you hold this book in your hands; please protect it and use the secrets of these pages to help this species. I will only entrust this book to a protector and loyal friend whom I have fought alongside, laughed, cried with, and willingly shed blood for. I have never hesitated to

*put my life on the line for this individual
or any other member of her family. I will do my
best to provide you with as many details and
a solid understanding of where you are and why
you are here.*

Out of the Jungle

It was April of 1970; the heat of the mid-day sun was stifling and hot with the elephant grass reaching well over eight feet high. I could hardly see the giant fiery planet; let alone two steps in any direction. I could hear the approach of cautious footsteps as someone crept towards me in the thick dense foliage. Whoever it was; the audible noise of the hoarse breathing and slow stealthy steps got louder as the space between us closed in. I could hear the unmistakable sounds of the dense undergrowth pulling at the hard wood stock of a rifle that I'm certain was poised and ready for defensive use. On my left knee and keeping low to the ground I held still and waited for the impending fight to come into range. There were two of them; speaking in low foreign tones as they scanned the area for US soldiers whom they aimed to put an end to. I controlled my breathing and quietly blew out my air down the front of my body as the sweat ran freely through my eyes and down the bridge of my nose. I blinked away as much moisture as possible but it continued to threaten my vision as I strained to stare forward looking for any kind of movement. Slowly, as if in slow motion, the outside edge of a small combat boot pressed cautiously into the soft earth within a foot and a half of my left knee. With steady hands I brushed my index finger lightly against the trigger and prepared for the imminent battle and waited out the agonizing seconds. The suspense in the air was thick and heavy as I stared intently at the boot that carried a soldier, much like myself; simply here to carry out orders from the higher chain of command. After what felt like an eternity, the heel slowly rose off the ground and stepped out of sight hardly making a sound. The distance between us had to be less than 24 inches, and the elephant grass offered the only concealment between me and a certain fire fight. My ears strained with anticipation, waiting to hear any hint of their presence or location; but only the eerie silence lingered, keeping me glued to my position for the next three hours. My partner, five feet back to my left didn't make a sound as we waited.

We had to get back to our camp; this was not what I needed just one day before I was finally leaving this god forsaken jungle. I had received orders to leave two days prior; the only condition was that I had to be at our supply drop off point at first light for my lift back to civilization. With a light piece of an old tee shirt wrapped over my mouth to keep from inhaling insects, I lowered my gaze to the ground and made sure that I could stand without giving away my position from the noise of the undergrowth. Tired, hot, and sore from kneeling in the same position for so long, we made our way parallel with the trail until we emerged out to the split in the route showing us that we were finally within a few hundred yards of camp. Taking my middle finger knuckle I knocked twice on the plastic stock of my M16 for identification and access to come into camp without having to look down the muzzle of the perimeter watch. Before I approached I knocked my knuckle again on the stock of my weapon and heard a response knock in the distance ahead of me. As we came into view I echoed a couple knocks and responses before slipping into camp. I was fighting the same stomach cramps that you get every Monday after taking the mandatory orange malaria pill. I know it's for my own benefit, but often times weighed the option of not taking the pill just to avoid the effects it had on my digestive system. Just ten yards away from my sleep area I got caught in another one of Vietnam's plentiful, 'wait a minute vines' as I stepped around an outcropping of bushes. These vines were heavy with thorns that literally made you 'wait a minute'; pulling and removing the sharp spikes before you could get yourself clear. They went through most plastic canteens leaving them purged of the clean water that you carried. Looking at several thorns now through my pant leg buried deep into the soft flesh of my calf; I had yet another reminder and sore souvenir to take back home.

We all quietly settled in to finish our last night among the elephant grass and swarming insects. In a small circle, prone with our feet pointing towards the center, I started the flame in my B-unit (Butane) stove and heated my water, along with my mystery meat rations that I managed to get open with my P-38 can opener. It was about seventy five degrees on that final night; but after acclimating to one hundred plus temperatures earlier in the day, I shivered as if I were weathering a blizzard under my poncho liner. Being in the central highlands outside of Pleiku; I could hardly wait to get into camp Enari and fly far away from the humid and treacherous jungles of Vietnam. Just before daylight I could hear the engine of the big bird coming. We were already up and more than ready to climb aboard the transport out. Stepping off the grass of that jungle and into the chopper was one of the greatest feelings I had felt in almost a year, just knowing the direction we were going.

With the wind in my face I looked out over the battle scarred jungle of Vietnam and prayed that the Huey I was on would make it all the way back to Enari so I could leave this jungle behind forever. The smoke billowing from her engine was blue at first but was now turning black and heavy in the swirling turbulence as we lifted from the damp green floor below. The blades were pounding hard to bring the heavy bus and cargo into a safe altitude for navigating through the contours of the mountainous area of extraction. Vibrations of the aircraft shook cargo and personnel deeply as we pulled up off the Earth's surface with the bittersweet smell of fuel and exhaust saturating our senses. This would be my final flight on one of these big heavy monsters and away from this wicked jungle littered with triggers and traps laying in wait for the next unsuspecting GI to pass. I felt a small sense of sadness to be leaving the familiar jungle behind; but also felt great relief as the pilot navigated further away from the hell hole where we had been pinned down for eleven straight days. There were only four men on board and I am confident to say that we all wanted to get as far away from Vietnam as quickly as travel would allow. Hearing rifle shots from the ground below and the sound of hot lead blazing through the metal shell of the Helicopter was an odd enough noise but surprisingly not one of us flinched. We had long since understood by the time you hear that sound, it's far too late to duck or move.

The thumping of the blades as they sliced through the air was loud and comforting as it meant only one thing; we're going home! The four of us sat quietly looking out over the green landscape as it rushed past, each lost in our own world and thinking of the lives that we would be stepping back into once we arrived back home in the states.

Mitchell, the youngest at about twenty, had left his father's hog farm in Ohio when his name came up on the lottery less than two years ago. Twelve months might not seem all that long but in the jungle of Vietnam; those twelve months played out like an eternity. With bright blond hair and long skinny features he towered over most of us in the platoon. One year ago he had a huge smile that couldn't keep his perfect, bright white teeth a secret; now his mouth was small and hard. We hadn't seen a glimpse of that smile since we touched down in the jungle in what seems like a lifetime ago. He had aged years and his eyes were dark and dim from the lack of sleep, nutrition, and what they had witnessed over the unforgiving twelve month distance of time here in Vietnam. His boots were dusty and had long worn through with cracked leather holes on the top crease; I wonder if he suffered from the jungle rot like the rest of us out here. His hands were worn and callous with the pinky and ring finger void of their previous existence on his right hand. His overall

posture was proud but worn down to a frag-
ment of what it was just a short year ago.
He was scarred inside and out, the twinkle
had left his eyes and was replaced with a cold
emotionless shell that reflected deep pain. I
hoped that he would find his way back to
his family farm and bury the memories of
this place deep in the fertile soil that existed
there.

Carter, known as 'Dog' was a little older
than me, possibly twenty-eight; the owner
of a country store in Nevada. He claimed
that one day he would have his own casino
and we were all invited to bring our money
through the front doors as long as it stayed
behind when we left. He was our 'tunnel rat'
and possessed that wild look in his eye as if
he had seen the secrets of the world and was
afraid of nothing. He always moved with
quick bursts of energy and talked faster than
anyone I had ever met. Dog was a good soldier to have around to pass the time, with
his endless bantering and continuous flow of
crazy stories. We called him 'Dog' on account
of the barking sounds that he expelled

within the tunnels that truly sounded like a canine whether he was coming in or out. Quick with any weapon; he preferred his bayonet over anything as it was quiet, which ironically; he wasn't. He stared out the window with a half-smile on his face, looking content and almost pleased with himself. Whatever memories he was hoping to leave behind in this deadly jungle were forever going to haunt him. He sat cross legged on top of his overstuffed duffel bag appearing relaxed and calm with his arms crossed in his lap. The veins throughout his arms were prominent and looked like a road map of a busy city. I couldn't imagine what was going through his mind right then, but I can guarantee that it was going a mile a minute. Throughout my tour with him; Dog never slept for long as he always woke up wildly flailing his arms as if to swim free of his horrific and vivid dreams.

Sitting directly in front of me was Kenneth Jackson, known as 'Jumping Jack' on account of his miscalculated emergency exit from a helicopter which was close to twenty five feet off the deck. The jump, or more accurately fall; was a result of gunfire that rolled the bird sideways to break away, and Kenneth simply dropped out the side entrance while unleashing a freefalling string of profanities. Kenneth was left mostly unharmed with nothing more than a sprained ankle and bruised pride. We caught up with him holding his foot just above the ground, jumping as fast as he could towards the tree line, it only seemed right to name him Jumping Jack. Ken was one of those guys that you couldn't help but want to be around, with his careful movements and calculated intellectual conversations. His voice was bigger than you would expect from a man his size, you always knew when he was in the room. He was the thinker of the group and had the unique way of telling a story that had you leaning forward in your chair so as not to miss a single syllable. When he told you about his trip to the gas station where he spilled gasoline out on the ground and all over his shoes; his narrative would have you laughing so hard that you might very well fall from your chair. He spent more time looking out for the needs of others long before he would even consider his own comforts. Staring down at his feet I knew he just wanted to get home and move forward with his new life that he would build for himself. His dark hair was whipping across his forehead and his jaw was clamped tight as if biting through the memories of Vietnam.

I was a local timber cutter from Montana territory who lived in a small two bedroom log home that I had built myself in the Bitterroot valley. With my sister and brother living in Missoula we had all grown up with very little, as our parents were in the timber industry with years of hard luck throughout our entire childhood. I never regretted those hard times or held my father responsible for the financial difficulties that we faced. He was one of the hardest working men I had ever known, and was respected in the valley as the man who always got the job done no matter how tough. I always hoped that they would be able to live a prosperous life with the wealth they deserved, but we lost mother to cancer in 1963. My father was lost just a year later in a logging accident. He had always been of the strong opinion that planes were too dangerous. My father would always say 'It isn't natural for a man to fly, if we were supposed to fly, we would have been born with feathers; a man needs to keep at least one foot on the ground.'

Losing his own parents to a plane wreck in 1961 was the worst possible way for them to go. My grandparents had the same strong opinion about flying, but found themselves on several 'business flights' with his work as a textiles representative. I'm certain that he swore how; 'he was always right about planes' on the final descent to the ground. The loss made for a tough couple of years for my parents as we found it difficult to keep up with their estate and the bills they had left behind.

After my own father passed in 1964; my sister, brother and I decided to sell off the house and divide the small amount that was left after paying off his debtors. We stayed in the familiar surroundings of Montana; close to the only family we knew, each other. I spent a fair amount of time with my brother before I came to Vietnam and could hardly wait to see him again. A couple of years back my 'lottery' number was called and I was fitted with an Army uniform and sent away into the unknown, leaving my brother and familiar surroundings behind. After one year in Vietnam, Dog and I volunteered for another twelve month stay; a difficult choice but we were weirdly connected to the fight. Looking out the opening through the doorway, the terrain had turned dry and dusty as we approached Camp Enari. The smells of real food cooking on a greasy kitchen grill and gasoline mixed with smoky exhaust filled the air as we approached civilization. This was the place where we were sure to find a hot meal, shower, clean clothing and a suitable place to rest. As the helicopter hovered just mere inches above the hard dusty surface the pilot jerked his thumb towards the open doorway and shouted "Get out, I'm going back in!"

Not needing a second invitation the four of us scrambled out onto the flat surface with blowing dust and thundering rotors barely above our heads. Bending over our duffels we ran towards one of the Quonset buildings, the giant metal bird labored skyward again with a deafening roar back towards the jungle.

Going from the damp moisture of the deep jungle to the dusty dry temporary military base camp made my nose run uncontrollably, I wiped the moisture on my shirt sleeve and walked toward the building. It felt great to be out of the jungle with the trip back home on the horizon. It had been two long years since I had been on US soil and I relished the chance to go back home to Montana and sleep in my own home. I missed the Bitterroot valley with its rivers and streams that offers some of the best fresh water trout fishing a man could hope for. Looking around for the chow hall; I needed food, hydration and a little rest before my flight out. As the rhythm of the helicopter faded away; the new sound of jeeps, soldiers talking and busy activity of the lively military camp took over. Their voices sounded loud and out of place; as jungle survival required silence and stealth. It was noisy and most comforting as the last few days were spent maintaining absolute silence. Crossing the dusty opening of a roadway I stepped into the dimly lit dining facility. With a quick nod to the cook I grabbed a metal tray, some silverware and approached the line for my first real meal in eight months. Ken was at my left elbow and playfully asked to see the wine list. With a quick smirk the cook ducked back into the noisy kitchen with the batwing style doors swinging behind him with a loud bang. Seeing the display of the various choices of food I couldn't help myself and was drawn to the basics of mashed potatoes and mystery meat stew. I felt that I was eating a fine meal prepared by the finest chef's on the planet and tried to eat slow so as to savor every delicious bite. I had forgot how wonderful a kitchen prepared hot meal could taste and promised myself another just like it when I got home to Montana. Ken ate his pasta with enthusiasm and seemed to float blissfully on every delicious bite. Dog sat across from us a couple of tables away and picked slowly at his food, lost in some dark heavy thoughts as he stared out the window.

I stood up to join him, but he put a hand in front of his tormented face and shook his head; he needed to dine alone right now, something we understood all too well. After a short time of pretending to eat, he stood up with his tray of food and set it on the counter by the dishwasher's window making a quiet exit. I finished my own food and excused myself from the table; something I hadn't done in years and headed outside to find Dog waiting in the shade of a nearby building.

"I can't leave yet buddy." Dog said with a shaky voice.

"Dog, we've been through enough don't you think? This is what we have been waiting for man; let's just go home and leave all this behind." I said firmly.

"Don't ask me why, I just can't leave yet." he said with tears starting to well up in the corner of his eyes.

"I won't ask why; but I will ask if you need me to do anything or take care of anything for you back home when I get there?" I questioned.

"I don't have anything that can't wait another year or two, I'm just going to have to stay here and work this out for myself."

After a long pause of staring out into the dusty road, Dog drew in a long heavy sigh and looked up with a weary grin. "Now go get yourself cleaned up before you head back to your family. The Army can't have you looking like a worn, torn bag of jungle mud on the flight home." Still lingering, Dog looked like he was struggling for the right words to say and a way to choke them out without giving up his composure. "You never failed me sir; might even say that I owe you my life on several accounts, but I'm going to have to face that jungle again before I'm ready to leave this mess and come home. Thank you,

Lieutenant Stone for everything; I'm proud to have served with you, sir." With tears in his eyes he stepped back with a crisp picture perfect salute which I returned with pride and a heaviness in my heart.

Dog turned on his heel and rounded the corner of the building and out of sight with the weight of the world resting heavily on his tired shoulders.

It took a while for Dog's discussion to sink in, but I think he made a choice that would suit him and maybe help him find closure. I believe that in his time here he found himself at a point of no return and he recognized that. He needed to find a path back home that he could live with; no one at home would understand what he had become and what it actually took for him to survive this jungle. Dog was mentally stable and wise enough to see that his responses and reactions that he had embraced in a war zone might not be a good match for civilian living. I had nothing but respect for Dog, and admired his strength and insight to make the hard choice. I never saw Dog again; but I will never forget the sacrifices he made for all of us out in that jungle.

My next objective was to get clean, change out of my filthy clothes and get some rest in a real bed. After a much needed shower and getting some clean clothes to put on; I settled into a starched linen bed which consisted of a twin mattress on a metal spring loaded bucking bronco for a bed frame. Tossing and turning for a half an hour taught me that I wasn't ready to sleep on anything that might move beneath me; so I rolled off onto the hard floor dragging my blankets with me and drifted off into a restless slumber. The constant noise around the barracks was too much to allow for any kind of adequate rest. The sounds of a jeep approaching, footsteps on the hard gravel surface, a whistle from a soldier; these sounds were tough for someone just coming out of the jungle to adjust to. Finally, I surrendered to the fact that rest would come later and got my things ready for the overdue, long noisy flight home back to the US. I was feeling anxious to get out of here and start my life over again with whatever sanity I had left. The 'Freedom Bird Flight' was assigned to leave in a couple of hours so I decided to just wait on my duffel bag out by the runway where the noise could take the place of the busy thoughts in my own head. It was no surprise to see Ken and Mitchell already waiting as if the flight might be late to take them home.

The flight on Flying Tigers Airline consisted of stops in Hawaii, Anchorage Alaska, and finally, Fort Lewis in Seattle where we were to spend the night and have a special dinner that would be served to us by new recruits that were headed across to Vietnam. The last leg of the flight into Seattle was bumpy, loud and seemed to take forever to finally settle down on the tarmac below. We were relieved with the final thump and screeching howl of the tires as they greeted the runway on American soil. It took only minutes to get off that plane and out into the open air of Washington. I knew in the back of my mind that the trees and brush didn't have the dangers of someone calculating the distance down the barrel of an AK-47 assault rifle. Even with that realization in my head, the need to be watchful of every shadow still hung over me heavily. Wearing my class 'A' uniform; I scooped up my bag and headed for the big metal 'Arrivals' building and the open exit on the other side. I was greeted by the recruits marching passed calling a familiar cadence and flooding the air with call and response tones that took me back to my initial enlistment days.

Out on the street, I pulled my bag over my shoulder and walked freely down the sidewalk with Ken at my side; proud of my uniform, my country and my service. The first few people we encountered were oblivious to our existence and briskly walked past without even looking up from their busy day. The further the two of us went, I realized that most everyone was consciously avoiding eye contact and a few even went to the lengths of crossing the street to the other sidewalk. I thought it might be that they were uncomfortable with the uniform and were not used to it. The truth was, that the war had been going on for a few years now and we were certainly not the first soldiers that had walked down these sidewalks in broad daylight. The reception was cool at best and the locals here maybe had their fill of the uniform and were over it. I was getting the idea that we might not be too welcome around these parts and felt the urge to catch the earliest flight back home to Montana where I could be around friends that I knew from my childhood. We were in for a long walk back to the air strip, only to be lengthened with the feeling of being an outcast and unwelcome. I was not about to hang my head or feel that my uniform was something I couldn't be proud of; I squared my shoulders and walked tall with my head held high, I was a soldier. The long dark shadows of the evening were daunting; just as unfriendly as the locals. The flight couldn't have come soon enough as we waited for our departure.

Ken looked over his overstuffed Military Bag and looked like the picture perfect poster of a soldier in uniform.

"Where are you going from here John?" Ken asked calmly as he lit a cigarette in the light breeze.

"I will be heading to Missoula Montana, then on to Florence, how about you?" I asked.

"I think I will head towards Salt Lake City and see what I can do with myself from there. I think it's time to get a college education and make sense of all this mess."

I looked down at his belongings and looked at his metal helmet secured to the side of his bag which was dented, dirty and showed signs of fatigue; just like the rest of us. Scribbled across the side of it in bold black marker were the words 'Running the Gauntlet' which was Ken's favorite catch phrase. These were the words that he would tell all the new recruits to help them get through the shock of being in Vietnam, 'You will get through this, right now you're running the gauntlet, but there is a light at the end of the tunnel, you just have to push harder than the rest.' I had gotten used to having him around as he seemed to be a wealth of information that proved to be most helpful over the last couple of years.

"Well buddy, I guess this is good bye for now; we will have to keep in touch and make sure to visit periodically. I'm sure I will need your expert advice when I try to build my new house." I said with a grin.

"You got it John, if you ever need any-thing; and I mean *anything*, make sure to let me know." Ken said seriously.

With a hearty handshake and a half hug, 'Jumping Jack' Kenneth Jackson gathered up his belongings and walked towards an open door. Walking a few steps ahead of him was Mitchell, also heading towards the exit and the final flight to familiar homeland. With a nod and a small gesture wave, the two walked out of view, leaving me com-pletely alone for the first time in two years.

My chest knotted up with anxiety and I found it difficult to breathe freely as the men I had counted on for so long were sepa-rated from me. Reaching for my own bags

I busied myself with finding my gate and waited with uncertainty for my flight to position in at the gate.

Settling into my seat for the flight home I started to feel confined and boxed in, as this flight wasn't an open fuselage like the old C130's. The area felt confined, stale and the air didn't seem to move as several of the passengers smoked cigarettes. I had never taken up smoking and having it all around me added to the anxiety of feeling penned in. The commercial flight was much smoother with cushioned individual seating. The stewardess seemed to understand my distress and kept the on flight beverages coming. Feeling the effects of the drinks, and exhaustion kicking in, I was finally able to drop off to sleep for a short time before the flight finally came to a halt in Missoula, Montana.

I stepped out into the open air in Missoula and was greeted by temperatures in the low twenties. The shock was breath taking as the cold air sliced through my lungs. Wringing my hands for some friction heat, I dug into my bag for something warmer to put over my already shaking body. It didn't even dawn on me that November was getting deep into the winter of Montana and the hot temperatures of Vietnam hadn't come with me. The crisp wind and snow-covered surroundings were the perfect distraction from the jungle I had left behind. The town had changed a good bit since my departure two and a half years ago when I was first called out to Vietnam. The mountains were clean, sparkling and covered in pure white snow that made you shiver at the sight of them. The direction towards the Bitterroot looked bright and crystal clear with a brilliant blue sky. It was time to make that call to my brother Bobby Lee and let him know that I was back in Missoula. I would also want to get my pickup truck from him and see if I could still drive in a straight line. Standing at the Missoula airport, out on the front sidewalk in a sun soaked phone booth I dialed Bobby's number.

"Hello!" Came a booming voice on the phone.

"Bobby Lee?" I asked; Bobby Lee had bright red hair and had been named 'Red' to those who were his friends; everyone else knew him as Bobby Lee.

"Yeah, who the hell is this?" asked Bobby Lee, not known for his manners.

"Your brother John, I'm in Missoula" I answered.

"Holy cow, where are you little brother? I'll come get you!" he asked not able to disguise his excitement.

Bobby Lee was twenty seven; two years older than me and had always referred to me as 'little brother'. He never got the call to go to war, knowing how he loved a good fight; I was even more surprised that he didn't run out and volunteer. I'm really glad that he didn't go; the experience might have changed him from the happy go lucky, care free man that he was. I loved his company and his loud voice that filled a room and seemed to draw a lot of attention; which was not always a good thing. On this planet, I wouldn't want anyone next to me more than my own brother in a bar fight. His head was thick, his words were sharp and his fists were thunder and lightning. Being a big strapping country boy he worked hard for a living and played even harder with a cold beer in his hand. He weighed in pretty heavily and looked like the slow moving country boy that might not get there too quick. That is just where most people underestimated the speed in which he could move; he was much faster on his feet and with his hands than I ever was. I never saw him back down from anyone or ever lose a fight; even when the odds were stacked against him.

One night he had three brothers mad as hornets at him over a game of pool they had lost fair and square. He not only played the game well, he had also earned some cash on the game along with the attention of the attractive blonde that had come in with one of the brothers.

It soon turned into an inevitable confrontation that would not end well for the trio.

With a huge smile he said, "Little brother, don't you dare get up out of your chair until it's over, no matter the outcome! This here's my game, that's my cash on the table and that purdy little blonde is gonna be my girl tonight."

That was the beginning of his 'tough guy' reputation as the guy who dropped the Olson boys all by himself. I remember that night perfectly as he had two of the brothers down with swift precision; he put his hand up in a gesture to the third brother to stop for a second.

In the suddenly quiet bar he reached over and took a big gulp of a beer sitting at a nearby table, set down the glass carefully and quietly; stepped forward to drop the third Olson brother with a flawless lighting fast hook to the underside of his chin. With the bar still silent, he grinned broadly with a loud burp and stepped over the unconscious brother towards me and said; 'This place is starting to bore me, let's get out of here and go find some excitement.' With a new blonde girlfriend on his arm, his crooked smile, and the way he walked out of that bar that night will always be the way I visualize my brother, Bobby Lee.

"I'm at the Missoula airport, just got in; sure would appreciate you giving me a lift, if you're not too busy right now, it's a little cold out here." I answered sarcastically.

"Oh boy, little brother; don't you move an inch, I'm on my way!" Bobby Lee instructed as he slammed down the phone in my ear.

He lived about ten miles away and if I guessed it right he was already heading for the door when the phone hit the receiver. That gave me about eleven minutes before he would arrive, just enough time to go back inside, get my bags from the baggage cart and get out of the building and into the parking lot.

I recognized his white 1962 Ford step side truck as it growled up the road towards me. The sound of the horn blew as my excited brother approached my position where I was sitting on my overstuffed duffel bag. The truck slid to an abrupt stop as the door flung open and big brother Bobby Lee rushed around the door with his arms open wide to embrace me with his famous 'bear hug.' Coming around the door on the slick roadway, Bobby Lee slipped a couple of steps but recovered before his balance got too far away. He looked like he hadn't aged a day since I left except for the fact that he might have put on a little weight, not fat, but thick dense muscle. Wearing dirty dungarees and an old black tee shirt, his collar length red hair was unruly and messy.

"Oh my, little brother, look at you; all spiffy in your uniform! It's good to see you all in one piece; come here soldier boy!"

With a wind stealing 'bear hug' my brother lifted me up from the sidewalk with a truly affectionate hug that only a big brother could get away with. It was wonderful to be here looking at him with his big loud voice and even bigger smile. You couldn't help getting caught up in his whirlwind of excitement and energy as he turned me in a circle and dropped me back to earth again with a hearty slap on the back. With my balance in question I put my hand on his shoulder and just took it all in with a big smile of my own. His mouth going a mile a minute he grabbed my bag and hoisted it into the bed of his truck and climbed in behind the wheel of the running vehicle.

"I've got your pickup at the house in the barn right where you left it with a cover on it. We are going to have to stop by the 76 station and pick up 5 gallons of gas for it; I might have to put a charger on that battery of yours." Bobby began.

"When is the last time that truck has run?" I asked.

"I used to go out and start it every week for the first year, but after not hearing from you for so long; it was kind of a heart break just to look at it. With all that crazy news about how things were going over there, I didn't want to think about it too much." he replied, "I got the packages you sent from over there, but I never opened any of them like you asked. I put them in the spare room with the rest of your stuff. Are you planning to stay a couple of days or just head down the valley right away?"

"I really want to get home; but a day or two here with you might be just what I need to get my bearings back. Is that going to be alright?" I asked.

"Of course Little Brother, you're always welcome at my house."

We drove on for a few minutes in silence as we fueled up the five gallon gas can and drove to his home. His house looked the same except for the second white station wagon in the driveway and a couple of kid's sleds in the yard. I noticed there was a young boy about four years old in a snowsuit on the front porch and a young woman of about twenty four standing in the doorway wearing a thick winter coat over her small, slender shoulders. The overall picture looked like the perfect family except that the girl on the porch was our sister; the boy was her son whose father had died last year in Vietnam. It caught me off guard to see her standing there with her son whom I had never met. She had moved away from Montana about five years ago back east to Virginia so she and her husband could start a family. I had not seen her since.

I did get word that her husband was deployed to Vietnam and subsequently had been killed last year not too far from where I was stationed. Without saying a word, I could tell that she was not at all happy to see me, and the look on her face was cold and uninviting. With a dry, unemotional face, she turned abruptly through the doorway and ducked out of sight. From inside I heard her call out to the boy who scurried across the porch and into the opening. With a quick glance from Bobby I could see that he had plenty to say but had held off so as not to spoil the reunion at the airport.

"I don't understand it John; she has it in her mind that you are somehow related to the loss of her old man. It doesn't make sense, none of it; I have tried to explain it but she's as stubborn as a flat eared mule." Bobby explained, "She'll not want to see you, or even let her son meet you. Believe me little brother, ain't nobody can get through to her right now."

"Does she only relate the fact that we were serving in the same country? There's no way I could have seen or even met the man. I haven't even had a chance to meet her boy; we're family Bobby. She's my flesh and blood sister and she doesn't want anything to do with me; that's not like her at all. We used to be close as kids; this war has torn my family apart."

"I know little brother, but Kim has always been head strong and hard on the entire Vietnam War. She even dragged that poor little boy of hers out to the airport about three months ago for a protest that made the paper. I have tried to reason with her but I know she's not hearing a single word of it. Let's just drive on out to the barn and have a look at that truck so she can gather up her little rug rat and head out to her own house. I don't want any kind of confrontation in front of her boy; lord only knows that he has been through enough as it is. I haven't got a clue how to get through to her and I don't believe today would be a good time for that particular conversation. Let's just get that ol' hot rod of yours a-rumbling."

Bobby Lee and I spent the next two hours kicking around the barn getting the old Ford truck running. It felt as if I had just left for Vietnam yesterday. We laughed about old girlfriends that we had and of course the ones that we knew were too far out of reach for the likes of us. He hadn't changed much in that respect but we had both seasoned quite a bit during my time away from Montana. After three days of playing catch up with Bobby Lee and trying to sleep in his quiet house, I felt that I had to see for myself the outside world and settle into my old familiar surroundings. I was anxious to get to my cabin in Florence and see if the two years had left me anything to live in, or if the angry squirrels had claimed 'eminent domain' and evicted me from my quarters. With my personal items stowed in the back of my pickup, I rumbled down the snow packed driveway watching my big brother Bobby Lee fade away in the rear view mirror. I felt suddenly alone and lost as soon as I rounded the corner and came up on Highway 93. Taking a right towards Lolo I realized that getting settled in meant that I had no military partner, squad or company, and it would take a bit more effort than what I had originally anticipated. The last couple of years I had grown to count on my military friends, knowing that I was part of something bigger than just myself. I knew in turn that my brothers in the military also counted on my presence and companionship just the same.

I found my cabin to be secure, dry, and just as I had left it except for the thick layer of dust giving everything that eerie gray aged color. The smell of wood smoke and cooking had long since faded away and been replaced with a stale, cold, and almost moldy dust. Opening the windows and doors allowed the cabin to welcome the vibrant fragrant mountain breeze back into the room and fill the cabin with bright sunlight. After checking the chimney for any nesting critters, I built a blazing fire in the stove to take the winter edge off the house.

The following three months flew past as I busied myself cleaning, dusting, trimming, cutting wood and digging my property into a manicured estate again. I stayed away from town and people in general as I found my comfort in being alone and getting used to an unrestricted way of life. I spent the following couple of month's snowshoeing the area, spending time up in the majestic Bitterroot Mountains and getting that feeling of nature and all the great things offered up on the high ground. Late in the month of April, I ventured out in the Selway area for an early fishing trip and all appeared to be quiet and calm. The only difference was the gut feeling that I was being tracked and watched as I made my way across the rocky slopes and summits of the grand landscape. The odd feeling never left for those few days which made me feel as if I was being a little too paranoid; but my gut feelings had never failed me before. This cut my trip short and I made my way back to the valley below and drove to the familiarity of my own home. You can never dismiss those kinds of feelings as our senses are more capable than we give credit.

Witness a protest

One evening in the beginning of May, the sound of a rumbling pickup truck coming up my driveway with the distant sounds of country music playing on the stereo interrupted my usual lounging around on the front porch. Rolling in with a cloud of dust was Bobby Lee in a clean, freshly pressed, button down shirt.

"Get in sweetheart; we're going to Missoula for some fancy dinner at the Oxford." He said playfully.

"Now that all depends on who's buying." I answered.

"We'll shoot a game of pool; loser pays." He said with a wide grin.

"Let me change my shirt and get my wallet." I said with a heavy exaggerated sigh.

The cool streets in Missoula seemed empty and quiet as there were fewer cars around than I remembered from a couple years back. Looking over at my brother, he looked intent on getting into the downtown area for a quick bite to eat and a frosty beer at the Oxford. The Oxford was known by the locals as the Ox, where he had been a patron for most of his legal drinking years. I didn't remember all the wrinkles around his eyes and the way he had aged, but it was working well for him. I don't think he had any trouble getting the attention from the ladies; the catch was to keep their attention for longer than a song on the jukebox. As we rounded the corner into the downtown area, there was a large crowd of people in the road with hand carried signs and the shouting was intense as we approached. I wondered if it was a parade or an event of some kind but as I read the signs; I realized that protesters were making themselves heard, voicing opinions against the war and the soldiers that were coming home from Vietnam. My older brother started revving up the engine and touching the horn on the truck to get through so we could access the road to the other side.

"It's ok Bobby" I said "let's just go around these lunatics."

"Huh-uh; no sir-eee, there's no way am I going to let these protestors get in the way of my day. I have the right to drive down this street; besides they are disrespecting all that you stand for!" Bobby Lee said with a tempered tone.

"I just got home a few months ago big brother; let's save the home fight for another day. I just want to get my hands on a cheeseburger and visit with my favorite brother for a spell." I said with a laugh.

"Oh heck John, I know what you're up to; I'm your only brother. You know it ain't much of a contest to be your favorite!"

Seeing his temper grow quickly I knew I had to keep this situation contained before it turned into a wild fight on the street in the middle of the Missoula town. Bobby Lee's shoulders were coming up around his ears and his white knuckle hands gripped the wheel as if his life depended on keeping the truck on its designated path.

"Let's just back out of this mess and go around, don't let them spoil our dinner plans. It's getting late so let's just grab a burger at the Ox and wash down the dust with a cold one" I said cheerfully.

"Doesn't this bother you?" Bobby Lee asked with a snarl "I mean, just look at them; all high and mighty with their signs and uptight opinions."

"Sure it bugs me but I think I'm more hungry than upset right now," I lied, "let's go get some of that good old Oxford grub buddy. Really; it will be lots more fun than hanging around here with this bunch of meat-heads. Besides, I haven't had a proper cocktail server to flirt with in a couple of years."

As he backed the truck through the lingering crowd, he seemed to let his tension fade as the distance grew between us and the shouting protestors. I know that he was angry on my benefit, and I was proud of that; but this wasn't the time nor the place to start a battle with the protestors in Missoula.

Big Brother, High Stakes

I had been home for about six months and had intentionally stayed away from family and friends for a while so I could get my head wrapped around the changes that I had been through and the changes in society. I never knew how anyone was going to react to me every time I came around the corner; I had maintained the 'high and tight' military haircut. I was proud of my service regardless of the rumors that hit US soil prior to my arrival. Maybe I just didn't want to hide that I was a soldier and paid attention to how others reacted to me without taking it too personally. Some would give a half smile and nod politely; others would literally back up, drawing their children close so as not to have any contact with the despicable soldier. I'm generally a good natured person but when I feel confronted by an aggressive person, I tend to avoid the mess of being confrontational, as my passion would get the best of me along with my instincts.

Finding a parking spot close to the bar, I got out and slammed the squeaky door on the tired Ford truck and headed for the front door. Getting settled onto a stool beside my brother at the Ox was just about enough to make me feel normal again, as we ordered our burgers and beer like we had in the years past. The bar was small but made up for its size with the busy activity of the down-town locals coming in for a quick fix of food or a cold beer to wash down the day's grit. My favorite bartender Megan was working behind the big solid wood barrier of the bar and gave a quick smile of recognition as we assumed the role of the weary, overworked, and underpaid patrons of the Ox.

"Hey stranger, I haven't seen you in a couple of years," then, turning to Bobby Lee she asked "you and your brother going to behave today or am I going to have to cut you off before you finish that first beer?"

"Aw, come on now Meg, we never create trouble in this here establishment, we're just trying to get by long enough to get some grub and take in the sights." Bobby Lee joked.

"Now what about you G.I., are you going to keep your big brother out of trouble long enough to finish that burger?" Megan asked playfully.

"I sure hope so; I've been looking forward to this burger for a long time." I smiled politely.

I always had a place in my heart for Megan with her shoulder length black hair and bright blue eyes. She had the whitest teeth I had ever seen, and when this girl smiled it took all the bad out of your worst day. When I had any kind of dialog with her, I bumbled along through the conversation, praying that I didn't say anything stupid in front of her. She was most likely the most beautiful woman that I had ever seen and that made for a very awkward conversation whenever I saw her. I tried to play it off but always ended up with my boot on top of my tongue and usually left the bar feeling like an idiot. Her good nature and care free personality made up for all my blunders and today I was relieved that the bar was too busy for much more than casual talk. I was content just watching her race around the room taking care of the growing crowd. With an elbow into my shoulder Bobby Lee asked if I wanted my butt kicked in a game of pool; which I obliged and lost four times in a row. The room was getting full and the energy of the patrons was getting to the point that I really wanted to get back to my quiet house and break away from all the noise. I am not anti-social, but I really wasn't ready for the growing energy in the room with the limited exits.

"Hey big brother, it's getting late, how about we get on out of here. I'm not quite ready for a crowd yet and I think it will scar me for life if I lose one more game of pool today." I said.

"You got it buddy, just let me settle up the tab and grab my coat." Bobby Lee responded.

As he made his way back to the bar, I settled into an open space against the wall close to the front door. Megan looked up over the noise and smoke to give me an amazing smile and wave that made me feel important for a brief moment. What caught my eyes were a couple of unsavory guys approaching Bobby Lee looking like they were up to no good. The first was a tall, wiry man in his twenties with deep, dark eyes and a flat crooked nose as if it had seen the impact of a few angry punches. His hair was cut high and tight in a military fashion, but there was no military demeanor. He only displayed the meanness and swagger of a guy looking to push his luck. The second was about the same build but had long shoulder length, greasy hair and a long gray coat with something poorly concealed beneath it.

The first guy leaned in and said something to Bobby Lee that changed his pleasant smile to that of cold hard anger. This had my interest piqued as I paid close attention to the body language of the two men. Bobby's face was glowing red in an instant as he spoke directly and calmly into the eyes of the first. Then he leaned around to the left and pointed into the face of the second and said nothing; just shook his head as if to let him know that this was a bad decision on their part to even come into the bar. Bobby Lee backed up a couple of steps; something I had never seen him do, and turned to walk away, only to have the first man grab at his right shoulder. Bobby turned quickly and placed both hands on the first man's chest and spoke again, too quiet for me to hear. I quickly pushed off from the wall and came in quickly to Bobby Lees left side. It brought back some old memories standing beside him like this; he was right handed and I was left handed. This was our design of staying out of each other's way when it came time to play rough with the other team. Whatever trouble these men had with my brother was now trouble with the both of us; and I was not going to leave his side on this one.

"Oh, look, Bobby's got company," the first one sneered, "Better go back to that wall before you find your worst nightmares come to life... boy."

I just smiled and stood calmly, keeping a close watch on the body language of the second man out of the corner of my eye. It's amazing when you look at one person directly, what you can see peripherally while you take in the whole picture of what is going on around you. The crowded room seemed to give a wide space for the four of us as the second man, slightly behind, shifted his weight to the concealed side; telling me that he was freeing up his right foot for a kick of some kind. The trouble with that, was the first guy shifted his weight to his right which put his hip and thigh in the path of my body blocking his partner from getting a clear shot. In order for the second guy to have any effect he would have to reposition his weight again which gave me all the advantage I needed as he began to move. I lunged forward into the first body pushing him backwards and to his right; with his weight baring on that leg, he had nowhere to adjust, resulting in him simply falling backwards into the chest of the off balanced second man. With arms flailing and left leg kicking high enough to grab, I simply elevated his foot fast and hard, increasing the speed and force of his fall. This put him into the arms of the second, who was not prepared to take on the extra weight or momentum, and both fell heavily to the hard floor.

Bobby Lee started to move in for the finishing touch but I reached out quickly and pulled him back.

"Not here; and certainly not now big brother," I said quickly "let's get out while the getting's good."

Not happy with the idea of walking away from a good fight and finishing his business. Bobby Lee reluctantly turned around and the two of us slipped out the front exit onto the sidewalk and into the cool nighttime air. Going left around the building, we reached the truck and I pulled the passenger door open and jumped in as Bobby Lee reached his driver's door.

The shot came from the sidewalk in front of the truck as the first bullet came through the windshield and out the driver's window, shattering the glass and entering into Bobby Lee's right shoulder who still wasn't in the truck yet. The second shot hit the hood and into the firewall. I dove into the front seat and made my way out the driver's door to put as much metal between the shooter and myself. As I came out into the open I reached back inside and pulled Bobby's .45 revolver out from under the front seat. As long as I can remember Bobby never went anywhere without that old pistol; he always hid it under his seat within reach. I hit the ground hard, crawling toward the rear of the truck where Bobby Lee was holding his shoulder. One look from him told me that his shoulder put him in a bad spot as far as backup goes.

"What the heck is this all about big brother, I mean why are they coming after you with guns a blazing?" I asked through clenched teeth.

"Gambling debt, and not what you think; they owe me!" Bobby Lee grimaced through the pain "They figure that if I'm out of the picture, they won't have to pay up."

"Are you kidding me? These idiots think they can shoot their way out of a little gambling debt?" I asked in disbelief.

"They owe me twenty two thousand dollars and the...."

The third shot came from the right and low to the ground. This time it went cleanly through the ribs of my brother and made a horrific exit wound out the lower back just above the belt-line as he slumped over quietly. I rolled under the back bed of the truck and leaned out from behind the tire on the opposite side with the .45 in front of my face. Directly above me was the second of the two men with a small sawed off shotgun in his hands looking past the tailgate for the two of us. Shooting straight up into the underside of his ribs I let two rounds go and immediately rolled back under the truck and out the other side to a standing position and moved toward the front of the vehicle. There was the other partner crouched low, looking down the passenger side of the truck getting ready to shoot again at my slumped over brother. Shooting two more rounds into center mass of the shooter, I stepped over him and rushed to the side of Bobby Lee.

"Get me into that truck and let's get the hell out of here" he said weakly.

Wrapping my arm around his ribs I felt the hot, sticky blood soaked shirt as I dropped the tail gate and helped him in. The familiar smell of blood filled my nostrils and took me back to my losses in Vietnam. This was different, as the blood I was smelling and feeling was from my own family, something I could have never been prepared for. I jumped into the back of the truck and helped him pull himself to the spare tire lying in the middle of the bed and let him wrap his arm into the center for stability.

"Hurry up before we get hauled out of here with county hand cuffs on." He said with a cough, pulling the keys from his front pocket and dropping them in front of me.

Hopping over the rail to the ground I pulled the door open and started the truck and backed out, driving over something big. I had a pretty good idea what it was; I put it in drive and gunned the accelerator and sped away, mindful of the precarious situation in the back of the truck. As I sped past the front of the Ox I saw Megan standing in front of the doorway watching as I drove by. The look in her eyes was calm, concerned and nonjudgmental as I raced down the street and out of sight. I drove quickly to St. Patrick Hospital emergency with my brother's life hanging in the balance. This visit would of course gather the attention of the local law enforcement, but the risk of losing Bobby Lee was well worth the cost of them locking me up. Coming to a stop under the well-lit awning enabled me to see in the back of the truck where Bobby Lee was clinging to a spare tire and his life. The amount of blood in the back of the truck was substantial and covered about half the bed. The first person out the door was an elderly gentleman I assumed to be a doctor, followed by a younger woman guiding a gurney through the broad glass doors.

"He's been shot twice and losing blood, please help him." I stammered in a hoarse voice.

"Is he a friend or relative of yours?" the gentleman asked calmly.

"He's my brother, he needs attention fast; come on I will help you get him on the gurney." I responded quickly.

"I thought so; hold on for a second and don't move him." the elderly gentleman said firmly.

He opened the tailgate and jumped into the bed of the truck and squatted down over Bobby Lee and pulled back some of his shirt gingerly and looked closely at the exposed exit wound. Looking up towards the young nurse he held up his hand in a stopping motion.

"Nurse, get some gauze, scissors, morphine and a few wraps, I need to hold off this bleeding before we adjust him in any way. If we try to move him like this we could be asking for trouble, his ribs are shattered."

I have seen plenty of bullet wounds in my military life; even seen men die from smaller injuries. With that much in your past you tend to become callused to the sight of it. Only today, this was my one and only brother; I couldn't just view this as just another battlefield injury. My brother Bobby Lee is all that I have left, without him I feel as though I would be lost.

The doctor paused for a second and looked into the gray face of Bobby Lee and glanced back at me with a concerned look that didn't hide the message coming with it.

"Son, grab his legs and help me get him on that gurney, we just lost the pulse!"

Scrambling into the bed of the truck, the doctor and I managed to get Bobby Lee on the gurney and rolling towards the door. He told me to move the truck to clear the lane and meet them inside right away. The blur that followed was chaos, to say the least, as I parked the truck and hastily entered the building looking for some direction as to where my brother was being looked after. The nurse behind the counter casually pointed across the hall towards a closed door with half glass. The pulled curtain gave a very narrow view of the flurry of action that was taking place as the medical staff tried to get a lifesaving heartbeat back into Bobby Lee.

There was an alarming amount of blood on the floor; the faces of the staff that I could see were serious and focused. I didn't feel the need to enter the room as my own expertise in the medical field was combat lifesavers course and held no merit in this professional arena. The I.V. beside the bed dripped continuously, the defibrillator was brought in as the paddles shocked the chest area for some hope of a stubborn jump start. Hearing the muffled "Clear" and seeing everyone raise their hands away from Bobby Lee; the final shock was administered. There was an eerie silence that followed and the down cast faces showed evidence that Bobby Lee was committed to rest. I couldn't feel my legs as everything in my body went tingly and numb. This was a moment that I did not want to believe; not even for a second. The doctor looked down at Bobby Lee with deep sadness that was sincere and heartfelt as if he knew him.

Time slowed down and sounds from all around went weirdly silent as the doctor looked up from the bed towards the door, where I stood in disbelief and horror. His eyes showed honest compassion and loss as he made his way around the others to the hallway where I stood.

"I'm sorry son, he lost too much blood and the internal damage was too severe to save him; this is a terrible loss; I'm truly am sorry."

Gesturing towards a seating area, he accompanied me into the room and sat across from me, leaning forward and speaking quietly.

"I'm not trying to get into your business son, but he was shot up pretty bad. I recognize him; been here plenty of times with broken bones and such. But he also sent plenty of patients my way too, with their own broken noses and bones. Your brother was one tough character who never backed down from anything. I will make his arrangements from here and contact you later; there is nothing more you can do at this time. I am not asking what happened, nor do I care. I just think that there will be a lot of questions coming from other parties and I don't want any interviews taking place at my hospital. Take that truck, clean it up, and get as far away from this building as you can, understand?" he stated more than asked.

"Yes sir, my name is...."

"I know who you are John, and I know where to find you, too. From what I know about your time overseas; I would guess you've seen about enough of this sort of thing. This kind of mess never looks good with the locals who stand with the protest signs; I can't imagine you need that kind of stress right now either. Trust me to clean up this situation, and get yourself in that pickup truck, and put some distance between us." He said with a firm tone.

"Thank you, Doctor." I said sincerely.

With a nod, the doctor stood up extending his hand, after a brief handshake, I briskly walked through the glass door towards the truck. Back outside the cool air hit my face and made me realize how still and stifling the hospital was inside. I never felt as confined as I did at this very moment until the pure open air of Montana filled my lungs.

Jumping into the driver's seat I drove straight for Highway 93 and towards my home in Florence. My mind raced a mile a minute as I rolled the distance away, in the dark hours of the morning. I can't imagine sitting in a courtroom trying to defend my actions in front of a panel of citizens who only see an Army Soldier from Vietnam. I couldn't even for a second, think that anyone on this planet would agree with, and not criticize my actions at the Ox; especially after leaving the scene. I don't see waiting in a holding cell for weeks, or even months, for those same people to decide my future. I know that I have strength and can handle most anything, but to be subject to the legal system that looks at me as a questionable character because of my military service isn't something I am ready to endure. I don't really want to; but the thought of leaving the state and far from this place might be my only option.

The Price of Sweet Revenge

It was odd to pull up to my home to see another pickup at my house, and even stranger to see Megan from the Ox sitting in the driver's seat waiting for me to arrive. She slowly rolled down her window about halfway and spoke through the opening in a strained voice.

"How is Bobby Lee?" she asked.

"He didn't make it Megan; my big brother didn't make it." I replied in a trembling voice.

The look that crossed her face was that of genuine pain and sorrow. Her eyes welled up immediately with tears as she spoke, "I'm so sorry John; but they will be looking for you, and they won't stop until they have found you."

"There were ten or fifteen people that witnessed the shooting but all they saw was an ex-military 'tripwire' that snapped." she continued, "It doesn't matter that they shot first, or that there were two of them. These people are sign carrying protestors who only have one objective; shred you in the courts. They won't see the fact that they shot your brother first; they will turn this thing into their own media frenzy and turn your military life upside down."

"It was self-defense, and I had no choice, there was no time to make any other decisions." I said scornfully, "I won't, and can't go to jail for protecting my family."

"You don't have much time John, before they piece it together and come to this house searching for you. You have to leave this place if you ever want to get any rest. It was easy for me to find you; I have always known where you lived." She replied.

Even at a time like this, her face was like that of an angel and with her eyes locked in on mine was unnerving, but her message was crystal clear; she had come here to warn me. 'Tripwire' was a name that was given to the Vietnam veterans that society had deemed unstable, and posed a threat to their normal civilian lives. Many of those disconnected soldiers had chosen to live out in the wilderness to escape the population and close-minded society that had shunned and deserted them. The men that slipped into the shadows of the wilderness, hunted, fished, trapped for food and settled into the wild. These men pretty much remained invisible from civilization; they were much more comfortable with nature, away from the judgment of others.

"When you leave, I promise that I will see that Bobby Lee is handled with dignity.

You just have to make sure that you don't spend the rest of your days in a prison." She said calmly.

"Did you know those men?" I asked.

"Only from the bar, not really regulars, but they stopped in from time to time. They got caught up in several pool games with your brother and were foolish enough to start betting each individual shot. I'm not sure what the total was, but by the end of the game they owed Bobby Lee plenty of money." she replied, "Now that would have been over a month ago."

"Was it only the two of them, or are there more that will be hunting me besides the lawmen?"

"No, it was only those two, they had a girl with them during the game but she got disgusted with the alcohol and losing streak and found her exit early in the night." she answered, "The Missoula county judge is a fair man, but he will be pressed to see this through the public eye, and be obligated to hand down some kind of sentencing. John you are going to have to leave, you know you can't stay here, both of those men are dead."

"Can you meet me here in the morning at 5 a.m. and drive me to Sweeny Creek Trailhead? I would not normally ask, but I honestly have no one else to turn to."

"Yes, of course I will be here in the morning. John, I am so terribly sorry!" she said with tears streaming down her cheeks.

"Thank you Megan; that will give me enough time to put a couple of things in order, and put together a pack."

She quietly backed her truck around and drove slowly down the grassy lane towards Florence. I watched her taillights fade away into the dark and sat for a short time putting together the whirlwind of events that I had just been through. There was no need to clean my vehicle so I pulled the truck up to the side of the house and parked.

I knew this would be the last time I would enter the threshold of my house, and the time had come to turn to the Bitterroot Mountains as my new home. I sat down at the table and wrote a few letters that would clearly outline what was to become of my possessions and estate. The house would be left to my sister's son, to do with what he felt was best, after the age of 18. I was going to simply have to disappear and embrace my new way of life in seclusion. I packed things for the long haul, but had to limit what I could carry on my back. I knew these mountains, and having to disappear would be no problem for a guy like me. Bringing only one firearm was a tough decision, but Bobby Lees nickel plated .45 was the only choice for this endeavor. I brought very few personal possessions but I did feel the need to bring a journal, my life would not be without record of the truth about this difficult night.

Bobby Lee and I had been brought up right; we never turned away from a hard day's work. We had been raised that an honest day's work, made for an honest day's pay. Bobby Lee and I had always been in the timber industry, thanks to our father. He

had grown up in Washington State working in the logging camps most of his life;
then moved us to Montana in 1949, but
continued to work the summer months in
Washington. I owed him everything for our
upbringing and the way he had brought us
up in the wilderness and prepared us to survive. I pulled down an old black and white
photo of him in his younger years at a logging camp in early 1909. His hard working
ethics and no nonsense take on life, was what
had made us strong; I missed him and was
glad he didn't have to bury his first born son.
Looking down at the only existing photo I
had of my father; his eyes were tired from
his day's labor, but they always glowed of
life and strength. Standing in the mountains
among the big timbers; his dark hair a mess
and a mustache you could hang a hat on. He
was a man always on a mission who never
gave up on anything. It was working in the
woods on a steep slope near Mt. Rainier that
had taken him away from our family in a logging accident. He had just finished cutting
a tree that turned and rolled back on top of

him; his buddies said that it happened too fast for him to jump to safety and played out so quickly that he was gone in an instant. The only consolation we had, was that our father didn't suffer and gave his life in the mountains doing what he loved.

I was going back into the wilderness; having this photo made for an easy decision; I would bring his memory with me on this journey. After deciding what else I was needed and securing my pack with enough ammo; I sat quietly in the corner of my living room, and just took it all in. I was lucky to have come this far, and have what I had. Stepping away was not the ultimate plan, but I was surprisingly very much at peace with it. Time ticked by at an agonizing pace as I thought about my night, and the months I had been back home. The events that led up to this point and the beautiful sunrise that was bringing light to a new way of life for me and what it was that I would become.

The sound of a vehicle coming up the drive confirmed that 5 o'clock was finally here. Peering out the window past the small sheer curtain; I confirmed that it was the same vehicle that Megan had driven hours before. Satisfied, I shouldered my pack, pulled my hat down snug and stepped out into the morning air towards the approaching truck.

Setting my pack in the bed of her vehicle, I opened the passenger door and sat down. Megan's face was tired and her bright eyes were dim from the lack of rest. I could tell that she had been crying plenty through the night, and she tried to smile through it all. Whatever torment she had put herself through the hours took nothing away from her raw beauty. With her hands on the wheel, she held her head low in an attempt to have her hair conceal her face as she backed the truck around.

"Where am I taking you, are you still set on the Sweeny Creek Trail or did you decide another trailhead?" she asked.

"Yes, Sweeny Creek please."

Quietly she turned the vehicle and headed back down my driveway. It was an awkward silence in which we drove back up Highway 93 to the Sweeny Creek road and ended up at the trailhead that entered into the wilderness. I couldn't think of a more beautiful face to say goodbye to, than Megan's. Handing her a set of keys and an envelope, I stepped out of the truck. I pulled my pack from the bed and was surprised to see her get out of the driver's seat.

"That's about 8,500 dollars; it will be more than enough to cover the cost of Bobby Lee's expenses and services. The keys to my truck and Bobby's truck, along with my house are on that key ring. I have well detailed instructions as far as the rest of it, whatever cash is left over I want you to keep for all your help." I instructed.

"The more I thought about it, I don't know you very well at all Megan, but I do feel that I can trust you with everything ahead. I know Bobby Lee thought the world of you and I have always had a good feeling about you as well. I am sorry to put it all on you like this, but from what you say, I don't believe that I've got much of a choice. I only ask that you keep this drop off point between us, and look after my brother's affairs."

"You can count on me for this John, I am truly honored to have known you and your brother." She said with a tear rolling down her face.

To my surprise, she leaned in close and kissed me gently on the cheek and stepped back. Her eye contact was pure and honest as she wiped the tear from her soft, smooth cheek. The slight hint of perfume and bar smoke could be detected from the distance; which is the closest I had ever been to Megan. This split second of time would forever be etched in my memory. For some strange reason it was the most beautiful smell I had ever experienced.

Knowing this was my cue, I shifted my heavy pack and turned towards the trailhead and began the one way journey up the path. I never turned back to look at Megan, I never heard the truck start, or the driver's door close. I can only assume she watched me leave until I was well out of sight. I struggled with the heartache, for the loss of my brother and felt the tears run down my own cheek as they cooled in the morning air.

Run to the Hills

Starting up the trail knowing that I was leaving all the familiar surroundings and comforts behind was an odd emotion that left an empty hole in my stomach. It was coupled with an unfamiliar sense of freedom that felt more burdensome than it did light. It was difficult walking away from the life of interaction between people and conversations. The feeling of loss for my brother and the position of knowing that society would imprison me if I were to step forward and face the consequences weighed heavily on my mind. It all seemed so unfair and the resentment began to build with each and every step towards high country. The feelings were mounting so quickly that I found myself pushing faster and faster up the trail as if to run from the growing emotions. Completely out of breath, I stopped in the trail and ripped off my pack and threw it to the ground in frustration. I could feel the emotion welling up inside; I had to sit down and think this one through. If I allowed it, this would cloud my judgment and consume my new life; I would truly be a slave to its negativity. I must get it straight in my head before I continued up that trail. I had to look at this as a turning point in my life and think of the pure life and adventures to come. I have always loved coming to the mountains and spending time, but have never been backed into a corner where it was not a choice for me. It had always been my own decision to come up into the high country and visit with the intention of coming back out to the comforts of a warm home and a hot meal with maybe a little social conversation.

My new objective will be to build my own roof and walls somewhere up here in these beautiful mountains and choose my own setting. I had no schedule, appointments or limits, that's how I needed to view this crossroad in my life. I still have choices, and control, I will not look at this as a punishment, but more of an opportunity to embrace whatever wonderful things these mountains have in store for me. It felt as if I had just been scolded by own conscience and been neatly put back in my place. With a slight smile and a confident new step, I hoisted my pack from the ground and continued up the trail with a renewed enthusiasm.

I aimlessly roamed the mountains for a couple of weeks, aware that the further I explored, the better I felt. I had fished many of the streams and found the high country trout to be plentiful and quite tasty on an empty stomach. I was looking for a place to settle in, call home and build a nice little cabin for myself. The entire range of the Bitterroot Mountains was at my disposal, and I aimed to find the perfect spot to stake my claim. I couldn't spend too many weeks searching if I wanted to be settled in before the snow came in, but I did have a little time left to do a proper survey.

Early one morning I had found a little resting spot on a hillside close to a game trail and settled in for a short nap. When I woke up I sensed that something was a bit off; I held still, long enough to listen for what had disturbed my rest. I heard movement and the sound of someone on the hillside, maybe 200 feet from my position. The labored breathing and clumsy movement of clothing was unmistakable against the dry undergrowth. Not leaving my spot I waited to see who it was, but the noise suddenly stopped and the movement ceased. The silence lasted long enough to make me curious to know if the individual had stopped for an extended rest or what had become of the visitor. I crept along the side of the hill when I realized that the person that I heard was now trying to sneak up on me; and was not more than thirty feet away at this point. He couldn't see me yet but I had a full view as he wormed

Footprints of a Legend
Pamela McKee

his way up the incline towards my last position. He was dressed in buckskins and had thick handcrafted moccasins on his feet. There was a wide animal skin belt around his waist with a large bowie knife and small pouch positioned on the center of his back. He was belly down on the uphill side of a fallen tree and was kicking up considerable dust as he awkwardly dragged his thick body alongside the dry ground. His arms and chest were deep against the dirt but his butt was elevated about ten inches off the ground as he pushed off with his knees and feet. He looked like a mountain man with long, stringy hair, dirty clothes and the overall lack of hygiene could be detected from the thirty feet that separated us. On his head was a fur hat that wasn't like a typical fur traders hat; it came to a point on top, instead of the flat round fur hats that I had seen in the past. He was doing a poor job of concealing his movements and it was comical watching him struggle with his lack of prowess. Placing my hand on the .45 for easy access I stood straight up in plain view and said, "Hey... up here."

His head came up abruptly, and looking my way, he came up to his knees with a surprised look on his dirty face. He had a long black matted beard with the entire left side covered in light dust contrasting the color.

"You a lawman?" he asked.

"Nope" I replied.

"Good enough for me." He said through a mouthful of yellow stained teeth.

Standing up quickly, he appeared relieved to be freed from his futile struggles. Avoiding any more eye contact he turned away without a word and ambled down the hill out of sight, periodically glancing over his shoulder towards me. His long dirty hair spilled out beneath his pointed fur hat and didn't seem to move with the wind or his movements; it was oily and stiff with dirt. He was a filthy man with a demeanor that made me uncomfortable that we were both in the same mountain range. It was no surprise that his only concern was that I wasn't the law looking for the likes of his kind. Lucky for me

I had no boundaries, and was looking over the mountains with my pick of anywhere I wanted to settle in.

I stood there for quite some time watching the hillside and saw him once again, he was much further away, working his way along the hill still moving down and away from my location. It was an odd visit, with such a limited dialog that it left me feeling uneasy with the whole idea. I didn't like the inclination that he was trying to get the drop on me. My best bet was to cover my tracks, keep watchful and also put as much distance as I could between myself and the direction he was heading. I reflected back on those last couple of days that I was in Missoula and knew that by now my brother had been laid to rest with a proper burial. I had to trust that Megan had been able to handle the difficult task and keep our discussion confidential as well. That part of my life needed to be put to rest, and I have to store those painful memories in a safe spot in the back of my mind. It was time to move forward and set my own path in these glorious mountains.

I covered a lot of ground over the next two weeks, taking in all the terrain, looking for that perfect spot to start setting up a permanent camp and think about building a cabin. My only dilemma was that every time I located the perfect spot; I would wander the area and find an even better location. That was the trouble with trying to find a great building site in such beautiful mountains. Every location boasted the perfect spot for settling. Each range whispered an offering and promise of tranquility, privacy, and abundance within its hidden valleys and undiscovered terrain. I was well into the heart of the Bitterroot Mountains, drifting aimlessly in and out of the Idaho Selway and then back into the Bitterroots of Montana. I felt that every horizon always had more and more beauty to explore. I just needed to make up my mind on a location of where I wanted to build a cabin before the winter months caught me without shelter.

Early one morning I watched several elk feeding out in an open meadow, just freely grazing on the mountain's plentiful supply of grass. Without concern, they periodically looked up from the deep grass to locate the others, then drop their heads back down, and occasionally adjusting the direction of the feeding line. The scene was picture perfect as I sat and enjoyed the distant company while they picked their way along the opening. The silence was interrupted by an unnatural howl that sent shivers up and down my spine as it echoed back and forth through the canyon walls reaching miles away. The howl resonated from a long distance from where I stood. That sound was like nothing I had ever heard in my life. The timber wolf has its own low, sad tone. They carry with their song a volume and lonely individual sound that can be recognized anywhere; but this was no wolf. The elk in the clearing jumped nervously and vanished towards the timber in a blur, leaving me alone and deserted in the silent wilderness. I had never witnessed this sort of behavior from the elk. I had never heard that kind of howl in all the years I had grown up in the wilderness and become familiar with the sounds, smells, and inhabitants. On that merit alone, a sound that was so far away and yet could still could spook the elk and send them running into the dense trees gave me pause. This should have given the indication that something out there was a serious force to be reckoned with. I had never heard such a sound. It was an eerie and piercing scream, yet lonesome at the same time. It was definitely loud, and had to have come from something large enough to emote that kind of length and volume. Whatever it was, it was big…really big.

I gathered my pack and headed over the summit towards a high set of cliffs in the distance that I had my eye on for the last two days. The rock outcropping was a great landmark and looked like a good location to scout for a cabin site as they protected the small clearings below from the worst of the elements. If I kept up my current pace, I could make it to the clearing by nightfall, my only hope was that there was a water source close by.

Throughout the day I would catch glimpses of the gray cliffs through the trees. The clearing and surrounding area seemed picture perfect for a spot to build my home. By nightfall I had only reached the bottom of the large clearing but the light was fading too quickly to really go any further without the risk of injury.

Setting up a tarp against a tree I settled in and built a small fire while listening to the night sounds, only tonight greeted me with dead silence and the normal comforting sounds of the evening were absent. The only time I remember the small animals and coyotes keeping silent is when a predator is near, and they don't want to be someone's next meal. Perhaps I was the perceived 'predator' and the animals were trying to figure out why I was in their back yard. It wasn't just the quiet, there was a distant and distinct smell of something 'gamey' in the air that added to the heaviness and unease. The silence made for a long night, I attempted to sleep but rolled around on the ground restlessly, knowing that something wasn't right out there in the darkness.

The morning sun was a welcoming friend as it pushed the darkness back into the west, the brilliant display of saturated colors and a welcoming warmth that helped ease the cold and restless night. Soon, with the deep red and yellow highlights burning in from the east, I could make my way up the clearing to the cliffs. I was fully packed and moving a half hour before the fiery ball crested the mountain tops and finished melting away all the nighttime shadows. The lengthy hike up the hill and through the clearing opened up into a much larger area than I had anticipated. The top section was bordered with several rock outcroppings that served as an upper boundary line. Beyond the rocks was a smaller clearing, followed by a little group of roughly fifteen to twenty trees in a flat, with larger rocky outcroppings directly behind, making the perfect wind block. There was an enormous rock slide facing the northwest just on the side of the meadow. Further up the hill to the right of the trees was a low ridge-line that looked promising. I made my way to the trees and set down my pack and stepped out into the open to make a better assessment. I could hear water somewhere above the ridge and was impressed with the view that rolled out in front of me.

Standing with my back to the trees I was looking out over the clearing at several mountain ranges that rose up out of the earth with jagged edges reaching into the deep blue sky. The ranges seemed to go on forever as far as the eye could see. The dark green blanket of trees covered the lower layer of the range followed by rugged cliffs and rock-slides, topped off with the remaining shimmering white winter snow and glaciers. Still facing downhill, to my immediate right was the vast rock-slide that rose up to the bottom of the cliffs that I had been using as my landmark for the last three days. Directly behind where I stood was a small patch of trees, a few cliffs and rocks that provided a great protection from the winters wind and snow. I turned left and walked uphill towards the sound of running water. I had gone maybe two hundred yards and crested the ridge-line to face a towering mountain of a glacier wall that had been in place since the beginning of time. This was an endless source of water, and the ranges beyond the glacier were equally as magnificent as the scenery towards the Northwest. The temperature dropped and was much cooler standing this close to the glacier, and offered shade from its sheer size. The side I was facing was easily 45 to 50 feet high and rose even higher the further back it went into the mountainside. The trickling water came from above the ice formation but flowed under a large portion of the glacier across the ground and down the side of the clearing disappearing out of sight. This was a perfect place to settle with a best case scenario with water, trees, protection from the wind, and views that took my breath away.

On the upper side of the glacier, I found the carcass of a mule deer doe that had mostly been devoured with the smell of the fresh kill still lingering in the air. The carcass lay neatly by the glacier on the rocks and had been stripped of most of its meat. What made it strange was the hide had been pulled back and the area surrounding the deer was spotless and untouched, there was no trace of scattered bones, puffs of fur. A pack of wolves would have scattered the animal and hair all over, as they feed and fight one another for the best portion. Only a man could be this meticulous and careful as to not allow the hair in with the meat. The meat did not show any signs of being cut with a blade, rather it was torn clean from the bones with sheer force. A third of the carcass still remained as if it were being consumed a portion at a time on purpose. Having it close to the glacier kept it chilled, which preserved the meat and kept it from spoiling for a much longer period of time. This had to be the work of some hunters in the area. This alerted me to stay on the lookout for possible company, hopefully not the unsavory type that I had already had the unfortunate experience of crossing paths with.

Coming back over the ridge towards my pack, I could not think of a better place to build my cabin and feel shielded from the elements and predators than right here within this small group of trees. With the rock-slide, the ridge line and cliffs; there was no better place on earth that I could call home. This was definitely the location where I would settle and build my homestead. I felt a sense of relief as I surveyed the area over the next couple of days. The location offered water, shelter, wood and sunlight, but was scarce with any type of wildlife. The truth of the matter was; I had not seen or heard any animals or found any sign of their tracks since I had arrived here.

Late one afternoon, I made my way back up to the glacier and knelt down to drink from the pure flowing stream that ran from beneath its monstrous form. The water was ice cold and had a taste that literally brought a smile to my face. Leaning down for another gulp, I saw some movement out the corner of my eye and it quickly melted into the trees to my left. Not getting a good look at what it was, I got my fill of water and made my way up the hill to see what kind of tracks it had left behind. The form was dark in color and had some size to it, maybe a deer or elk; it didn't really matter, as long as there was game in the area. Standing in the location that I was certain the movement had come from, I stared around my feet at the untouched ground. A little mystified, I started circling the area looking for any tracks whether they be hoof prints, or bear tracks, just to make sure I wasn't just seeing things in the daytime heat, but still found nothing. I couldn't place my finger on it, but there was an odor that was hanging in the air. It wasn't a familiar smell, but it held a sharp unforgiving stench to it.

Shrugging it off, I went back to where I had left my pack and began scraping out a nice level spot for a modest sized cabin. The next several days were spent clearing away much of the underbrush in the area, and figuring out what trees were going to work as cabin logs. I didn't want to take the trees close to the cabin because they provided good protection and shade.

Realizing that I had my work cut out for me, I headed uphill to search for my cabin logs. I'm not a lazy man; but knowing that I would have to drag them to the site I would much rather drag downhill than fight to carry them up. Work smarter not harder I thought to myself. In my haste to leave I did have enough foresight to bring a one man saw for cutting trees but was kicking myself for not having thought to have also grabbed my ax. This was going to make splitting wood a real challenge but I had some ideas for that. About a mile and a half away I found a nice creek, it was narrow, but deep, and provided some of the best fishing I think I have ever seen. There were many days spent finding the perfect logs for my cabin, but I would switch it up periodically and take advantage of the incredible fishing. It was as if the fish had never been exposed to an angler up here so high in the mountains so getting a quick dinner made my life easier.

On one of my fishing days, I caught three pan size trout and began cleaning them on a sandbar. Suddenly, a softball sized rock splashed down in the calm water no more than five feet away from where I was kneeling. I was in a small, shady, flat area, with nothing above where a rock could have accidentally fallen from. The incident startled me and sent me sprawling backwards into the grass, and sent my fish sailing through the air only to land back into the water. With only tree branches above, I could only assume that the rock had been thrown by someone nearby trying to scare me away.

Quickly scanning the area, I removed my pistol from its holster and rose up slowly on one knee waiting for anything to move, or seem out of place. I came up on my feet and stood still for a few minutes, waiting for any kind of sign, but saw and heard nothing at all. A little unnerved, I reached down and scooped up my fishing materials, two remaining fish, and backed out of the area trying to make sense of what had just happened. One thing was for certain; I didn't take kindly to someone trying to scare me off this mountain. I thought back to the mountain man that I had encountered a few weeks prior and considered the possibility of him being in this area and trying to mess with me. By the time I got back to camp I was starting to get pretty mad about the whole thing, wondering if that greasy haired grub worm was trying to spook me out of here, away from my new found home. If this was the case, than it was time to go on the hunt myself and turn the tables on this nasty critter.

Once in camp, my pack caught my eye; it had been pulled apart, and the weeks' worth of logs were now scattered out in the clearing below. Quickly, I went through my pack to take an inventory of what was left of my possessions, carefully combing through the contents and found nothing missing at all; not even my food, or hunting knife. An animal would have eaten the food, a man might have taken my hunting knife or something of value, but every last item was still here. It was as if the only harm done, was that all my things were carelessly strewn over the ground. The logs were scattered, but were moved no more than twenty feet from their original location. This didn't make any sense at all; if this was not the work of an animal, than it had to be that nasty mountain man trying to get under my skin, and it was working. I circled to the backpack where I had cleared away the shrubs and made my camp fires over the last couple of weeks, looking for his moccasin tracks to verify that he was indeed, the culprit. What I found stopped me dead in my tracks. I was looking at the tracks of a barefoot man, only much larger than that of any man I had ever known. The track was almost four inches longer than my boot and wider by two inches. The tracks were clear in several spots through the dusty areas, but vanished into thin air once they hit the grass. A man with a footprint this size would have easily reached seven feet tall. I had never witnessed a track this big, let alone one that was human. That familiar pungent smell filled my nostrils and reminded me about the time above the glacier. Was there a giant barefoot man up here in the wilderness, or was that creepy mountain man pulling out all the tricks trying to make me look foolish?

Living in a Tripwire Hell

The next two weeks were spent preparing more trees for the cabin and staying close to camp so I could keep a watchful eye on my things. I couldn't shake the feeling that someone was observing me as I went about my daily activities. I remained vigilant searching for anything out of place, and those footprints in the dirt certainly weren't helping. At night I would hear wolves howling far off in the distance; it made me uncomfortable thinking about them finding their way into this area. I continued to check on the deer carcass every couple of days and always found it undisturbed, until one morning when it was completely gone. I don't mean just eaten, but completely gone; fur, bones, meat, fat, the entire carcass. It was so clean, there was no trace that it had ever existed. Finally this made sense to me; it had to have been hunters that came back for the rest of their deer meat. I did find it bizarre that they took the bones and hide as well, typically hunters will leave the unnecessary weight behind and not carry it out of the mountains.

In the short time I was away from my camp investigating the missing deer carcass, I returned and was greeted with a completely ransacked campsite again. This time my pack was scattered over an acre of land, and all my logs had been thrown down the hill from where I had been positioning them for the last two weeks.

With my anger peaked and my campsite a disaster, I cut loose with a bit of a temper tantrum and threw my emptied backpack down the slope with a loud "Son-of-a..."

Never finishing the sentence, a foreign noise stopped me dead in my tracks, I realized I hadn't spoken a single word out loud in several weeks. The sound of my own voice seemed strange, so far out in the woods.

I had become a non-speaking, disheveled, dirty, confused, hermit, pack throwing mountain man; and it didn't look good on me.

I paused for a moment to gain a little perspective; first off, why did I go through all the trouble and throw my pack down in the dirt? Looking around the grand surroundings, did I think that my lack of self-control and mini tantrum would have any impact, even on the smallest scale? My deficient hygiene and greasy hair didn't make me much different than the nasty mountain man I had run into a while back. Aside from all the mess, I knew that singing, whistling or speaking would help keep me grounded and focused. Unless of course, singing and speaking to one's self, while alone, is the first step towards insanity. I had already constructed a little outhouse out by the small cliffs, and desperately needed to get this cabin up and under roof before any adverse weather came. Even though the logs and pack were tossed all over the place, the outhouse always remained untouched. That alone was something of a mystery to me.

I went to work dragging the trees back up the hill and stacking them onto their perspective piles. Again, nothing had been taken from the backpack, but my aggravation was beginning to build and I didn't care much for dragging the same logs back to camp for the third time. This time there were barefoot tracks in the dust and I was able to distinguish a couple of different sizes. They were big like the first one, but one set of tracks was just a shade smaller than the other. It would have taken several hunters to do this much damage in the short amount of time I was gone.

Hoping they were still within earshot I shouted, "If I ever catch you in my camp, touching my things, somebody's going to get hurt!" The threat was weird, as I saw and heard nothing, in fact, I'm convinced that I am the only one on the planet that heard my voice. Had I just taken my first step toward insanity?

The entire next week I scrambled to get more trees cut and started to 'box' in my cabin. I pushed through a hard day and put five rows of logs up before settling in one night. I assembled a rickety makeshift bed to keep up off the ground and placed it inside the walled off area. Tonight I wanted to sleep in my split room mansion in the making. The walls were barely high enough to keep the breeze off while I slept on my elevated bed, but it felt like I was actually in a civilized home for the night for the first time in months. The open skies and stars from horizon to horizon were always a welcoming view, and I took great comfort in having solid walls around me.

I had been asleep for no more than a couple of hours when a scream, sliced through the night jolting me out of my bed and scrambling for my pistol. The scream lasted for a solid fifteen to twenty seconds and flooded the dark with its haunting volume and depth. It echoed for what seemed like an eternity, fading through the valleys below. The sound came from just down the hill on the other side of the rockslide, much too close for comfort. I pulled on my boots, wrapped my blanket over my shoulders and returned to my bed, only to sit upright and alert for the remainder of the night. Sleep had eluded me, gun in hand, I was prepared for the worst. The haunting sound had a howl similar to that a wolf, with lungs of an elk, and the scream of a mountain lion. It was loud, not the kind of loud that hurts your ears, but with volume and depth, enough to echo and reach miles away, even long after the sound had stopped. It sent shivers down my spine, and the hairs stood straight on the back of my neck. I kept replaying that unfamiliar sound in the back of my mind. This was similar and seemed related to the howl a month or more ago when I was watching the elk in the meadow. Never had I heard anything like it; this sound had a much deeper tone to it, sort of sad, lonely and tormented.

Daylight finally arrived and with it offered a slight cloud cover and cooler temperatures, it was easier to push hard through the afternoon heat. After elevating three more layers on the outside walls of my cabin, I felt proud of my progress, the building was now close to chest high. I was ready to treat myself to a couple of fish, a bath, and a quick exploration around the other side of the rock-slide. I needed enough fish to supply me with food for a few extra days so I could finish my walls and begin to set the framework for the roof.

At the stream, which was about forty minutes away, I was able to catch seven nice trout in less than an hour. After a brief cleaning of the fish, I settled into the water for a chilly, but exhilarating bath that was long overdue. Sitting in the two feet of water I completely submerged myself and scrubbed at my hair that was growing much too long for my standards. The hair on my face had taken over and was harboring some dried leftover food during my last feeding frenzy. Bathing was not as much a priority since I was alone, but the fresh renewed feeling reminded me that I had better set a regular schedule for my personal hygiene and add it to my list.

As I rose up out of the water, two black objects moved to the left of where I was and disappeared out of sight into the trees. With my eyes still filled with water, I had no way of really seeing what it was, but passed it off as a bear with a cub, or a moose with its youngster. The event didn't bother me, I have always known that I am not the only creature out here in these mountains. It would have been easy enough to dismiss, until a rock came hurling down into the water, almost hitting my elbow. This was the second time I had almost been struck by a rock near the water; this was no coincidence.

I can't recall a time in my life when I moved faster gathering my things and scrambling down a trail. I needed to separate myself from the stream head back toward camp. Running like a lunatic without a stitch of clothing on, I scurried up the trail with clothes in one hand, and boots and fish in the other. I could only imagine what I looked like streaking down a mountain trail with the dust sticking to my legs and a string of fish slapping my thighs with each stride. I stopped after a half mile to dress; I tied my shoes and finish buttoning my shirt, when I heard the sounds of knocking on a tree as it bounced against another in the wind. This might all seem normal, except there was no wind at all. The sound stopped after three distinct knocks, followed by two just like it no more than a couple hundred yards in the opposite direction.

This kind of signaling was familiar from my time in the military, it made me uneasy, not knowing who or what was making the sounds. We always tried to mimic the natural sounds that occur in the wild for our own communication. If this was that mountain man from months ago, things were about to come to a head. I refused to get run off, nor was I going to live in fear of anyone out here in my new home; this was my territory.

I was watchful on the trail behind me as I left the area, scanning for any kind of movement or sound. I made my way back to the bottom of the rock-slide looking for any clues that would reveal who or what was tracking me. This section of the clearing was going to be time consuming and difficult, the ground was mostly rocks and could take hours of scouring in hopes of finding some kind of print. I decided to return to the cabin, fry up all the fish and get back to work on my home. The rock flying into the water was no mistake, I needed to be more watchful and make sure I'm not vulnerable like that again.

Reaching the cabin site, things didn't get any better at all. The work I had put in over the last couple of days had been pulled apart and scattered like match sticks back down the hill. I can't be sure what all came out of my mouth at the time, but let's just say; I was a bit unhappy and my burst of profane dialogue echoed offensively back and forth through the mountainous wilderness. My logs had been removed all the way down to the soil. I did not want to deal with this destroyed cabin and hated the thought of having to start from scratch, carrying the logs back up the steep grade; for the fourth time.

In the three hours I was away, someone or something had managed to scare the dickens out of me, and sent me running naked through the wilderness like some kind of a wild mad man. Here at my camp, someone else destroyed a weeks' worth of assembling, and left me standing in the ruins with seven dusty trout in my hand in need of another cleaning. I stepped back and noticed that my pack had been untouched; which at the time I counted as a small victory, but the rest of the damage was beyond description. I mumbled a few more colorful adjectives; better left unheard, and went to work dragging logs back up the hill again.

If this was going to be a battle of will power; well, they just messed with the wrong man. I had enough logs and food to get the job done, I was not leaving until I had all four walls and a roof framed up. By nightfall I had one row of logs back into place and the rest of my materials re-stacked beside the foundation. I set my bed back inside the outline of north wall simply out of defiance to sleep inside my cabin. The night was clear and cool as a light breeze whispered its way through the trees. I was tired, frustrated and sore but the star filled sky above reminded me that my worries were small and insignificant. The universe wasn't going to wait or feel sorry for me, my life was actually, pretty great. I smiled as the fatigue settled in and I dozed off to sleep, these little bumps in the road only made my life more interesting.

The next three days and nights were busy assembling my home and remained fairly quiet and uneventful. Never leaving the site, I was able to get all four walls up with a small room divider in the middle. This would put my ceiling inside almost eight feet high to the cross structure for the roofline. It wasn't going to be fancy but it was my home and needed to be cozy. I had my doorway ready with two window openings for ventilation but built two solid shutters so I could close it in tight. I positioned my bed and settled in late one night and started planning my roof work for the next day. The distant sound of thunder filled the air and the smell of rain approaching woke me up inside my sturdy little open air fortress.

I was still two or three days away from finishing the frame work for the roof, and another day or two beyond that from being dried in. The rhythm of the gentle rain came in softly and grew into a continuous pounding of a relentless downpour.

The rain fell nonstop for two and a half days holding me hostage; soaking and sulking on my waterlogged bed. I realized that what I should have been building all this time was a giant wooden boat. I was thankful for the door being cut in already; I'm sure the cabin would have filled with water and set my solid wood bed afloat without a means for the water to escape. The only thing that stayed dry was my pack that was hung up on one of the walls with my poncho liner over it. Everything else, including me and my bedroll was were soaked, muddy, cold and miserable. Several inches of slippery mud remained on the floor for days after the rain had stopped. The next two days I pushed mud out the door and tried to clear away the endless built up pools from around my cabin. I was able to find enough flat rocks from the nearby cliffs to make a stone floor in the cabin that would prove to be a luxury once I got my roof put in place. I worked on the roof for the next five days and made sure that there was no easy way for water or unwanted rodents to come inside. The rip saw and I were getting a serious workout from all the long planks that needed to be cut and the blade was holding up better than me. The end result was a solid roof that made the cabin feel like a sturdy bear proof wooden fort.

Finally under a sealed roof, I sat on the wooden bed and surveyed the inside of my cabin. This was home; my very own homestead, and I was proud of the final product. I had a small, short wall, dividing the room in two; separating my sleeping area from my eating, storage and preparation area. My poncho liner, wool Army blankets and food supplies were going to have to last me a lifetime. There would be plenty of hunting and food rationing to get me through the harsh winter months ahead. My journey, which had gotten me to this point had been a difficult challenge with many unexpected setbacks. Sitting here, right now in my little fortress was everything that my existence had amounted to; life was pure, simple and perfect. All the odds were stacked against me settling in here, but either sheer will, or stupidity, had gotten me through. I was here to stay.

I built a few work benches around the building so that I could put game meat out for jerky and dry the hides for winter warmth. It will be a nice home to return to, after all the hunting and fishing I expected to do over the years. I stopped at the back corner of the cabin and looked uphill over the cliffs and back towards a massive rock-slide.

I noticed the movement of something large slipping into the trees. Trying to get a better look, I stepped to the right and noticed several more objects close, also dropping back into the shadows. I never really was able to see anything for sure, and shrugged it off as several elk that didn't want to be seen by the only human on the hillside. I had been here long enough and made no effort to conceal myself, all the wildlife on this side of the mountain knew where I was staying. Elk, deer and bear would graze close, but kept a safe distance, and vanished if they felt threatened.

Unsavory Mountain Men

I had been put through the ringer trying to get my cabin put together, and the end result was a great little home that would protect me from the rain, wind and cold winter months that were approaching fast. I had enough short lengths of firewood to get through the freezing months ahead. I had started a saw cut on one end and was able to split the wood with wedge shaped stones beaten through with my makeshift sledge hammer. It made me smile to think I was evolving back into the caveman days with the exception of my outhouse. This structure was private and hidden in the trees with three walls and a solid cliff overhang roof. I had designed a lean-to positioned over a twenty five foot crevice in the cliffs that loomed a couple hundred feet away from my cabin. It was deep and narrow; the hole was small and I was able to pour enough dirt into the opening to make me comfortable while being sanitary. I was always appreciative that the bathroom had never been pulled apart; maybe not worth the effort or simply just one of those things that's off limits. I wonder if I had marked my territory like a dog or coyote would, even if it was just my outhouse.

The weeks to follow were spent hunting out beyond the stream and into the thick wilderness for an elk that could feed a guy like me through the winter. Not once did I ever come back and find my cabin messed with again, even the contents inside the walls remained untouched. I believe maybe I had passed the test of survival and been allowed to stay here in this mountain for the time being, maybe in hopes the winter months would drive me away.

Hunting elk in the high country is no easy task considering the terrain you will have to cover to get you and 900-1200 pounds of meat back to your dwelling place. There were two nights up in the high thick growth areas about six miles above my cabin site where I had spotted a nice herd of elk moving towards the direction of my cabin. Smiling to myself I wondered if I should just head home and wait for them to pass by my front door and save me the effort. My little smile disappeared when they all collectively turned away and moved quickly over the ridge-line and out of sight with no sign of slowing down. Something had spooked them away, long before I had a chance to get close enough to shoot. I had heard the howls of the wolves in the area but had not had an opportunity to cross paths with any of them. I wondered if it had been the wolves that had spooked the elk.

It was time to venture out and away for a better idea of the land that I called home; so I packed enough food for a few days out and headed down the hill towards the distant ridge-lines. It was tough going through some of the rocky areas; all provided hidden basins of thick dense trees and signs of elk and deer beds. The wildlife seemed scarce close to my cabin site but the further away I traveled the more animals I ran into. About two days travel away from my cabin I broke camp one early morning and was wandered through a small cozy basin that had a small trickling stream of ice cold refreshing water. I looked beyond the trail beside the edge of the stream and noticed numerous moccasin prints in the soft moist dirt. It had been months since I had seen any sign of humans besides my own boot prints; it actually caught me off guard as it hadn't occurred to me that I was not the only person in this mountain range.

"Howdy Stranger!" came a voice not more than twenty five yards away on the opposite side of the stream.

The sound of a human voice was startling and seemed to come out of thin air and put me immediately on the defensive. Following my instincts; I dropped to one knee in the water and crouched low pulling my pistol from its holster scouring the trees.

"Easy there stranger, I'm right up here; no need to start shooting!" The voice came again in an attempt to sound friendly, slightly above me.

Looking up towards the sound, I observed a leather clad long-haired man in his mid-thirties looking out from behind a large pine tree with his empty hands held out in a non-confrontational posture. He was smiling behind a matted beard that showed signs of food that had missed its mark during his last meal. His shoulder length hair was oily and matted but his eyes told a much different story than the big smile that he so boldly tried to hide behind.

"You startled the heck out of me; I thought I was all alone up here." I said standing back up making no effort to holster my weapon.

His eyes were small and dark with a look of a wolf about to spring on its prey.

"Well, you kind of caught me off guard too buddy; you just passing through or are you looking to set up a camp?" he asked with a touch of antagonism.

It felt strange to hear his voice and respond back as I hadn't had a conversation with anyone in months; I believe I had grown more comfortable and accustom to the silence. I also have a tough time with someone calling me 'buddy' whom I have never met and had no idea who I was. Kind of a pet peeve of mine when someone does that and hasn't earned the right to call me buddy.

"I'm just headed over the ridge-line and back out of here." I said shortly.

"You all alone up here doing some exploring?" he quizzed.

"We've been up here for about a week, just doing some exploring." The use of the word "we've" was the intent on misleading his question about me being alone.

His eyes shifted slightly to the bank behind me as I heard a small sound of movement high above my position. Turning I saw a small branch that was still moving from something or someone passing by but nothing else was in sight to confirm what it was. Looking back across the stream, the filthy little mountain man was still positioned behind his large tree but now had his hands resting on the front of his belt; one thumb inside the waistband and the other resting on the handle of his large Bowie hunting knife.

"I guess I had better be on my way." I said calmly, still holding my weapon in my hand.

"Yep, I reckon." he replied with a twisted grin, once again exposing his yellow teeth.

Turning I glanced back up the bank behind me; certain that there was someone else in the brush, I moved downstream into the thick brush and dense trees. Once I had gone about a mile and a half, I cut back upstream at an angle that would put me well above the bank and whoever was on that hillside.

Footprints of a Legend
Pamela McKL

Only now; taking the time to move silently and making every move count, I used all the cover that nature provided to get back on top of the hillside unseen without leaving a trail behind. I moved quickly but carefully upwards until I was positioned a half mile above the stream where I had the encounter. Sitting above the area I was able to see the whole picture and watched as two leather clad mountain men were working their way down the stream where I had just gone. I recognized the second one as the dirty mountain man that I had seen on the mountain side months ago; he was still wearing that distinctive pointed fur hat. They were tracking my movements downstream, if they had any skills whatsoever they would soon realize that I had doubled back and now had the upper hand. I spent two more days wondering aimlessly further out and away from my cabin; this time intentionally leaving easy to read sign of my trail heading towards civilization. I knew that my followers were too curious to just shrug it off and assume that I was just passing through; especially since one had seen me at a different time-frame months ago. It was now time to vanish without a trace; I left the area after crossing into a rocky dry creek bed making certain that I left no evidence of the direction I was going. It took two days of only stepping on rocks and sweeping surfaces behind me to cover my path. I felt certain that I wanted nothing to do with these two mountain men. I had always relied on my gut instincts, and they told me that nothing good could ever be gained by associating with those two unsavory men.

Finally returning to familiar territory I felt a great sense of relief when I came up over the rise below my cabin and saw my home. It was a sweet feeling of being back to my safe place where I belonged. Unlatching the door, I pulled off my coat and set down my pack on the dry floor. I unlaced my boots, pulled off my socks, laid down in my bed and fell into a deep sleep to rest my tired bones; I was finally home.

Close Call with Creature

A couple of quiet weeks had passed since my run in with the dirty mountain men, and I must admit; I didn't miss their company one bit. I had been hunting all day with no luck and was heading back to my cabin when I got a most pleasant surprise that would make my life comfortable through the winter. I was less than a mile away from my home when I heard something on the trail running hard, out of breath and moving fast towards me. I quickly stepped off the trail and into the shrubs only seconds before a cow elk came running down the path at full speed and would have certainly plowed right over the top of me. Her tongue was hanging out from exhaustion, her neck and back wet with sweat; she had been running long and far enough to wear her down. As she labored past my hiding spot, I carefully stepped back out on the trail and fired a single round. This was such a lucky gift that had me smiling from ear to ear, setting my winter food at a full supply.

The lone shot rang out loudly and seemed out of place so close to home, but the end result was much needed. The odd part of it was, this was the first time I had fired a shot since I had left civilization. There was a bitter sweet feeling that came with the shot from the weapon; the food it would provide, but the memories brought back the loss of my brother. He would have approved of this cabin, location and conditions of life I had chosen for myself. I thought of Bobby Lee often and his memories carried comfort and joy as I recalled the years of our wild childhood.

It took the entire day, packing meat back and forth over the mile of almost level ground. I had really been given a gift from the wilderness after weeks of hunting with no luck. With a heavy fur blanket, I should be able to stay much warmer during those upcoming cold winter months in the cabin. I had no more vandalism issues while away from my cabin once I got the roof finished, the doors hung and windows covered up. With my wood piled high, water so close and meat supplies in full stock I was looking pretty good for the months ahead in seclusion. I spent the next week catching as many fish as I could fit in my pack and brought them back to the cabin for cooking and storage up by the glacier for now.

The glacier proved to be a great place for food storage as I had carved out foot and hand holds in the thick solid ice mountain and climbed up about twelve feet. Being high off the ground I had carved out another two foot by four feet wide 'ice box' deep into the frozen mass to protect my food from possible hungry animals.

I packed the fish on the left and elk on the right in some edible leaves and vegetation for my greens fix over the cold months. I had placed a few woven branches into the mouth of my ice box to keep away the birds that might fly close enough to see my food supply; it was a perfect elevated refrigerator. It looked like I had an adequate supply of food and wood fuel for about seven or eight months. This should be enough to carry me through, even if I became snow bound and couldn't go anywhere. I had snowshoes to build and plans to use them through the entire winter months for some small game trapping. The plan was to stay active and busy trapping to ward off cabin fever.

I was just coming back over the ridge from stocking the shelves of my natural refrigeration unit when I caught a glimpse of something dark with a red color. It was moving fast through the trees and running away from my cabin. My first thought was the culprit that had been ransacking my cabin before I finally got it built; but when I saw it clearly moving through a small open area I could hardly believe my eyes.

It looked like a small primate; at that distance it was hard to tell how tall with deep red hair and was running like a person. I had never seen a monkey that ran upright on its legs like a human being. It was thick and heavily muscled and ran fast and fluid like an Olympic athlete would sprint towards the finish line. This thing was moving in a very upright fashion, not a typical primitive knuckle using movements with bent knees, but the same as I would run or walk. In the few seconds that was all I could catch; it moved quickly into the trees and disappeared without a sound.

I walked out to where I knew it had run, looking for tracks and found human footprints that matched the size of my own barefoot track, only a bit wider. I have never known of gorillas or apes to be part of the western Montana wildlife; no, this was something that must have escaped from a circus or zoo somewhere. There was an unfamiliar heavy, musky skunk stink that hung in the air that was almost nauseating. I had not spent enough time in the proximity of monkeys or gorillas to know their scent, but it was all starting to come together now. That would explain the eerie howls I had heard previously. I was disturbed by the fact that it ran in an upright position, but even more interesting was that I had seen similar tracks but on a much larger scale. The possibility of several gorillas in these mountains seemed a bit farfetched; but it would explain the tracks. I didn't see the creature too well, so my only reasonable explanation was that someone was trying to scare me away from my cabin; that would be the most logical conclusion for the upright running. But why go through all that trouble all the way up here in the in the middle of nowhere? Standing here questioning the event and doubting myself was starting to give me a headache and I thought it best if I just went back into the cabin and rested for a while.

As I came around the side of my home towards the front door I ran straight into another gorilla. The creature was crouched low by the wall, as if inspecting the walls of the cabin. Surprised by my intrusion, it turned towards me with its outstretched hands and swung a closed fist towards my face.

In a defensive movement I grabbed the knife from my waist and slashed outwards while trying to get my footing well enough to retreat back around the corner. The blade sliced hard, in a fast downward motion into the head of the beast in front of me running almost the entire length of its face. With a loud scream it reacted with a swinging motion as it struck my forearm and elbow with its oversized hand, sending the knife bouncing off the outside wall of the cabin into the grass. I had backed myself against the wall with my pistol pressed between my waist and the wood structure out of reach.

With my elbows straight I was holding my hands in front of me in a defensive position waiting for the impending attack. In an instant the blood immediately covered the face of the primate and it swung blindly at me, this time hitting my neck and jawbone. There was a flash as the impact rocked me into the rough surface of the wall with my face bouncing off and my knees buckled from under me.

Too stubborn to give up; with my vision hazy from the blow, I pressed forward and grabbed hold with both hands and got my hands around the thick neck of my attacker. I pulled myself in close and drove my thumbs deep into the soft tissue of the throat still trying to clear my foggy head. As I squeezed harder, the fist rose up again and came down hard on the side of my face; splitting my cheek open with a jolting blow; but I wasn't about to let go. For that split second I looked into the face of the gorilla and couldn't believe how human like its features were; he appeared young like a teenager. His head was cut from the top of his eyebrow through the length of his face reaching to the side of his mouth with blood running down his chest and over my arms. His deep set eyes were wide with fear and surprise as he stared back at me with what looked like the big brown eyes of a person. It was startling as I looked at features that were more like a hair covered man instead of the primitive ape-like nose and wide mouth. He was maybe two inches shorter than my six foot frame but his strength was at least two times what I possessed. I would not be able to hold on much longer as he slowly raised his hands for another strike to my skull. What hit me next came in fast and hard from behind, and the daylight and sound instantly turned off.

When I regained consciousness, I was lying face down on my chest with my knees under me, my rear end was up in the air; my arms were at my sides and my face was half buried in the dusty earth beside the cabin wall where I had fallen. This was the kind of position that an infant might sleep, but not for an adult that was bleeding from his face. I had just been smacked around by some angry prehistoric caveman with an attitude; this was not my idea of an adequate or comfortable resting position.

It took a great deal of effort to get unfolded from the dirt and get back up into a normal standing position. I could tell that whatever struck me from behind had put a sizeable split on the back of my skull that was now soaked with blood. Placing my hand down to feel for my pistol, I leaned up against the building and looked over my surroundings with a very careful eye. I only hoped that the danger was gone and I could make my way to the glacier for some much needed ice and a thorough clean up. Convinced that there were at least two of these gorillas out here in the woods was not something I wanted to encounter again without a little distance and my pistol in hand. There was no way I could physically handle another hand to hand confrontation with one of them, let alone two. After a difficult struggle to stay balanced without falling down I made my way up to the glacier. The cold water and ice to the back of my scalp helped the swelling but the pounding headache was raging in full effect and showed no signs of letting up. It was time to tighten up the cabin windows and door and turn in for an early night.

That night it rained until late morning and left the following several days overcast and gloomy as my injuries throbbed and my body complained through the healing process. Three days after the attack I had slept soundly throughout the entire night, finally feeling some relief from the wounds. I was surprised to find fresh footprints around the back of my cabin close to the wall where I slept. I had heard nothing in my slumber and wasn't too keen on the idea of visitors coming around without me knowing. I spent the rest of the day setting up 'tripwires' around the perimeter of my cabin that would give me better warning when someone or something was near. Putting up the tripwires was a reminder of the life I had left behind in the civilian world. My life as a timber cutting man, the life in Vietnam, the homecoming and my brother who had been laid to rest because of a foolish wager on a pool game, was now here; in this mountain range. The phrase 'tripwire' seemed more fitting than ever as my actions might be construed as paranoid or hyper vigilant. The perimeter that I set up was to keep me informed of any unwanted company whether I was away or when I would sleep at night.

That night under the full moon I was awakened by the sound of another long shrill howl that seemed to linger on for minutes as the echo's called back and forth in the cool, still air. The rest of the night was quite except for the sound of something on the rock-slide down below the hillside. I wasn't in a position to go investigate the noises and sure didn't want another run in with the tough little furry, fighter twins in the darkness. I thought it would be best if I stayed right here in my solid little fortress of a home and tried to sleep. The sounds of the movement lasted all night and prevented me from getting any real rest. I had given up on sleep and before long I was staring out the small window crack anxiously awaiting the first hint of light. By the time the sun came into view, all the movement outside had ceased and I was too tired and sore to go snooping so I drifted off into a restless slumber.

The following days were spent looking for tracks, signs or indications of what had been out here moving at night. The open field showed a lot of pressed down grass and rough areas in the soil that had been disturbed but no tracks in the green carpet that revealed anything solid. I wasn't up for climbing over the rise to pick through the rock-slide area hoping to find anything more. The facts were; I was not alone up here in the wilderness and I was going to have to be more attentive so I didn't get bludgeoned by any of the hairy, fist wielding gorillas. The season was changing and I was going to have to go out and find one more big game animal for back up food supplies and thick fur to ward off the cold snaps that were closing in.

My plan was to go over the ridge past the glacier and hunt well above the cabin so that bringing the meat home would be a downhill drag and much easier to manage. I crossed over the ridge and walked to the glacier, looking up the side of it admiring my clever frozen ladder and hiding spot for meat supplies when I saw the bodies of four elk lying close to the ice. They had been placed there deliberately to stay cool and were lined up neatly in a row. The interesting part was that they had not been cleaned or skinned; or shot for that matter.

They had been hit with something to bring them down; clubbed in the head was more accurate. I have hunted elk before and to get close enough to club an elk was just something the human is not capable of. They had also been carried here, not dragged or quartered which was absolutely mind boggling. My run in with the mighty monkey men was enough to convince me that their strength was well beyond their size, but to carry an animal this big would take something twice his size.

Then it occurred to me; the other, much larger set of footprints that I had seen in the dirt at my cabin site. Could it be that there were bigger beasts out here of the same species? This could mean trouble for me, especially if they wanted inside the cabin with size like that. There was no way I could defend myself against something that big; I would even question how effective my pistol would be in that case. Looking at the elk carcass made me question how they could have gotten here without being butchered first, but unable to picture how it was even possible.

I turned away to head up the hill for my own hunt when standing in front of me not more than twenty feet away was a giant gorilla like creature standing like a man. I stood in shock, never even thinking to grab my pistol as it turned and faced me squarely. Its arms hung loosely at its sides with a large dirty elk antler in its right hand. Not moving it simply stood and looked me over as if to try to figure out if I was a danger to him or possibly a food source.

This creature was male with thick sloped shoulders like that of a power lifter. His legs were long and thick like tree trunks and bulged at the calves like he could run over the next three mountains before getting winded. From where I was standing he looked to be close to seven and a half feet tall; overall he looked like a man through his body features but his head had a slightly sloping forehead with a hint of a cone shape to the top of his skull. His brows were thick and his nose was small and flat like that of a boxer with a wide square jaw line that ran into his thick broad neck and shoulders. The hair that covered his body from head to toe was jet black with hints of gray showing on his chest and head. The most amazing feature was his piercing blue eyes that looked back at me with solid confidence and absolute fearlessness. I could hear his breathing as his great lungs smelled the air to gather information about what and who I was. I didn't need to draw in such a deep breath to catch the scent in the air that surrounded this huge beast. It was that same pungent skunk type nasty smell that I noticed and was becoming more familiar. I stood motionless for about two minutes as we sized each other up and took it all in; the notion to go hunting today had completely vanished as I looked at this magnificent beast. A noise caught the attention of both of us as another beast of the same size came into view with a small elk calf hanging across his thick shoulders. As he came in behind the first male he stopped short seeing me for the first time. With a loud blow through his nostrils he ducked forward and dropped the calf elk on the ground and backed into the trees with amazing speed. Still calm and composed, the first male took in one more long breath of the air and turned slowly with his back to me towards where the second had disappeared to and walked calmly into the trees and out of sight. I was completely dumfounded at this point; how in the heck could this be happening? Had I been up here too long and starting to see things that weren't there? Was this the second step towards my insanity?

Laying on the ground in front of me was the carcass of a young elk; I walked up to and kicked it lightly with my foot. Yep, it was real, and the smell in the air was real too; the bitter sweet nauseating skunk smell that I had encountered before. I needed to go back to my cabin and try to put this all together in my head. My impulse was to run frantically to the safety of my cabin and try to piece all this together, but I was completely in a daze. Walking back to the cabin my head was spinning, this thing showed no fear of me and allowed me to see it without even shying away. Was this something that I was going to have to get used to? Was this the creature that I had heard of from the Patterson/Gimlin movie from 1967? I remember this movie and was skeptical like everyone else, but still intrigued at the possibility. Everyone seemed to be taken back by the footage of the film, and like everyone else I was one of the biggest skeptics. I had seen the hand held shaky movie and thought it was nothing more than a publicity hoax. This particular hoax was looking back at me. The height, muscular build, hair and smooth stride as he walked away was much too familiar. Was this a real live 'bigfoot' right here in the mountains of Montana?

No More Hiding

There was a strange calm stillness in the air as I came out of the cabin. The next few days I tried to hunt and gather winter supplies and act 'normal'. The feeling that I was being watched was undeniable. I made an attempt to follow different patterns and change up my routine so as not to become too predictable in my own behavior. Not too certain why I was doing this; I decided that I wasn't the one that was hiding but the one that was most exposed to anything and anyone who cared to see what I was doing. Early on the fourth day after seeing the large male by the glacier I came out my front door and saw two of the creatures standing in full view of the clearing. They were looking toward the cabin and to me and my dumbfounded expression as I stepped out into the sunlight. There was no effort to move or shy away as I stared at them; much to the contrary, they simply returned to look for berries and edibles in the undergrowth as if I were not even there.

I attempted to do my daily chores of stacking my firewood from the previous days and straightening out the rest of my outside area. I caught myself pretending to be busy with my head down but my eyes kept darting towards them. What a couple of incredible creatures as they were both about the same size; one male and one female. Their physical appearance was that of an athletic muscular human; only much larger and denser by comparison. They ate and fed close to each other; both were between seven and eight feet in height. The male and female had powerful sloped shoulders with bulky but highly defined arms and legs that looked capable of handling just about anything. Side by side the female was actually a hint larger than the male and barely showed a more feminine outline as she moved and dug away at the brush. Her face had a more slender appearance which pronounced her strong wide jaw line and high cheekbones. The forehead on both was a bit taller than a human and rose up into a slight cone like fashion. The males face was narrow around the eyes with an exaggerated brow line, more of a primitive look around the eyes but the cheekbones were high with the same thick wide jaw. The whole primate mouth was not at all the case as their lips and mouth were identical to that of a human. Their posture was the same as mine as they walked upright and bent down to pick at the underbrush. The hair that covered their entire body was black with hints of brown; it was not thick or long, but similar to that of the common monkey. They too spent a large amount of time watching my actions and behavior but unlike me made no pretense of not being interested. The search for food led them down and away from the cabin and eventually out of sight at which time I went back inside to lay down and try to process what had just happened.

I spent the rest of the afternoon outside just hoping for another look at the incredible species I had seen earlier. The casual demeanor of the couple didn't present a threat and I hadn't even thought about being in any kind of danger despite their unnatural size. I saw nothing throughout the rest of the day but the feeling of being under a watchful eye was overwhelming; and the pungent odor hung in the air. The next day I thought I would be bold and venture out in the direction of the glacier and see if the big game was still there. I hadn't even gotten fifty yards from the cabin when two beasts sprang from the trees through an opening and scurried up the hill and out of sight. They were both smaller than the couple I had seen the previous day, one black and the other had a distinctive deep red tint to it. They moved quickly but not at a fearful pace as I had seen before but slow enough for the black one to turn back and look at me as he distanced himself. I recognized this one from the encounter at the side of my cabin as the critter I had cut deeply with my knife. I couldn't forget that face; especially with a blazing red full length scar running down his right side. That split second of recognition was obvious, followed by a look of aggravation before he turned away and vanished into the trees. The one with the red tint slowed down to a complete stop and looked directly at me, squaring off with a fearless arrogance that showed both confidence and disdain. I felt that this one held the grudge much deeper than the one who had actually been cut. He paused as if he had all the time in the world and wanted me to know that he was not at all afraid or hindered by my presence. He was more thick and dense than the other; the shoulders sloped sharply up into the base of his skull and gave no real definition of where his neck began or ended. His eyes were smaller and protected by a solid thick brow line that gave him a mean, scary look.

This made six different beasts that I had seen in this area, leaving me feeling a little bit crowded with population and I wasn't sure were even going to be good neighbors. At this point I really had no choice but to make the best of it as my commitment to winter here was already established. It was just a little hard to adjust to the idea that I was living within the territory of a Bigfoot population that up to recently I had passed off as a fairytale myth full of hot air. The Patterson/ Gimlin film had me thinking the real truth was right in front of me and my skepticism had completely been washed away. The next few weeks were filled with casual sightings of the couple, the two smaller males that I am guessing to be youngsters and the magnificent black male that I had seen at the glacier.

One sunny afternoon I saw two more that were quick to fade into the trees I had not seen before, they were both females and large full size creatures like the couple from the clearing. They had to live close to this cabin, but as to where exactly, I hadn't a clue as they were always on different sides of the cabin and moved away in the most direct line away from where I was. If they always went uphill or downhill that would help me pinpoint where they stayed but for now I was content with the fact that they always wandered away from me and not towards me. It was comforting to know that I was not alone in these mountains but it still remained to be seen whether or not these beasts were going to be kind neighbors or just sizing me up for winter food.

I was heading uphill towards the glacier to pick out some of the fish that I had stashed in the ice, when I came face to face with the two young males on the trail. One had a large crimson scar the entire length of his face that I recognized right off the bat and the second was his companion of similar size and age with a red tint, almost a deep glow to his hair. The three of us stopped, facing each other with curious inspections from me to them and vice versa. I stood stiffly with my hand resting on my knife and brushed my hand over my hip where my pistol should have been; but in my complacency, I had left it at the cabin on the foot of my bed. I tried not to show any fear or intimidation, but not having the pistol as a backup had me feeling open and very vulnerable; especially given our violent history.

Seeing the two standing still side by side and shoulder to shoulder was incredible; they looked like heavily muscled men in size, but their faces; also very human like, resembled that of teenage boys. They were both equal to my six foot height, but thicker and more rounded with broad shoulders and dense muscular legs. Every inch of them was covered in hair but not thick like that of a long haired dog but thin like the others. Both had a thick solid brow line with the familiar longer forehead coming to a cone like appearance on the top of their heads. All in all, they were magnificent specimens of whatever species they represented; I would have to tolerate and grow accustom to the idea that they were Bigfoot. The male with the scar dropped his eyes to my hand resting on the knife and his eyes narrowed in recognition. The scar showed a little more brightly as his eyes came back up and met my eyes in a steady look of preparedness, but still fearless. It looked as if he was calculating whether or not he wanted to lunge at me or wait for a better time, from what he knew had injured him in the past. It was the red one that chose for us as he just started walking towards me as if I were just another useless object on the trail. The same trail that I now stood in the middle of. Not wanting to show weakness and give all the space, I stayed on the trail but moved only six inches to the side to make room. He literally brushed my shoulder as he walked by with his steady hard eyes looking at me with disgust. It was then that I got the full effect of the pungent nasty odor of this filthy animal as it made me cough as he brushed by. The sound made his partner with the scar jump and his posture tightened up as he made a wider circle around me as he went past; not bold enough to make contact with my shoulder. I held still and turned my back to them to resume my walk towards the glacier as if their presence didn't affect me at all. The truth was that I was shaking with adrenaline as if prepared to fight, which I have no doubt, would have ended in my abrupt loss.

Walking away was the only thing I could do to disguise the tension in my body and my shaking hands as the distance between us grew. I thought I was going to explode with excitement as I finally made it out of sight to the glacier where I guzzled down volumes of water. I'm guessing that my presence was something they were getting used to, and the hiding was over for them. My money would be on those two young males, as the culprits who threw the rocks into the stream and destroyed my progress as I was trying to build my cabin.

The next three weeks progressively got colder as the leaves in the valley below had turned to golden patches of color through the green landscape. There wasn't much in the way of 'sightings' as I rarely caught one of the beasts out in the open; and even then I was ignored as they carried meat, tree branches and shrubs over the hill towards the rock-slide. I guessed that they lived close by and were collecting their own winter supplies. I had no inclination to follow anyone of them to see exactly where they lived; I felt it was better to stay out of their way as I was the outsider. The sightings came to a complete stop after the first lengthy freeze; in fact I can't say I blame them due to their lack of clothing. My guess is that they hibernated like a bear and were trying to sleep the time away.

The first snow hit and salted the mountain with a three inch blanket of white beauty that pronounced a contrast in the contours of the mountains. The color didn't stay long as the next week brought fifty and sixty degree weather for two days; but the storm that followed made the statement that winter was here to stay. I had not yet had any time to build a fireplace inside the cabin so any cooking and warming up all had to be done outside beside the front door. It was the only way to dry my frozen and wet clothing and cook for myself. I really missed the comfort of cooking and staying warm inside my four walls. When summer came back I would make it my mission to build a nice stone fireplace with another lean-to for firewood storage that would keep it all dry. All in all this was a great place to be living and my first winter went well, considering the amount of time I had to put this cabin together. I had finished my snowshoes and provided my first opportunity to try them out in the two and a half feet of snow that came down. As I made my way to the glacier I found that I needed to make a few adjustments to my snow shoes; nothing that I couldn't take care of in an afternoon. Climbing the ice ladder I took out a small portion of meat and filled my coffee pot with fresh water and shuffled my way back to the cabin keeping on the lookout for my neighbors but saw nothing. There wasn't a trace of any tracks in the fresh snow as far as the eye could see; what I had forgotten to do was take in the scenery of the surrounding mountain range with its new clean beauty. Stopping at the front door of my cabin I turned to breathe it all in with a renewed interest; this would be the first of many winters in my mountain home. I promised myself that I would start taking the time and appreciate the surrounding beauty and witness its seasons with respect and interest. I was living in a paradise of rugged scenery with some of the most interesting neighbors; this was a great new beginning.

My winter proved to be uneventful and surprisingly quiet on my side of the mountain with snow falls that at one point reached seven feet high. I kept a trail mostly clear throughout the winter with my snowshoes and continuous trips back and forth to the glacier for water and food supplies. I cannot be certain that my roof could have taken the weight of the deep snow so I always kept it brushed off. At one point I had enough snow on the ground beside the cabin that I could walk level from one side over the roof to the other side. I think my first winter went well considering that I still had months of firewood left when the melting snow started showing signs of the dirt beneath. The quiet little trickle of water that ran beneath the glacier was now a loud flowing stream that gurgled muddy runoff water from the elevations above. I began to see signs of tracks in the snow when the temperature started getting above freezing; but the snow was still piled high at our altitude. The first set of tracks other than my own were a single set of tracks that walked a direct line from somewhere towards the rock-slide. The tracks came roughly ten feet from my trail and stopped. The male or female must have stood for quite a while as the snow had melted a good bit from the heat generated from their bare feet. The impressions were deeper by a few inches than the tracks walking up to that point. The side by side feet had turned to a perfect set of hard ice footprints before turning back around and following the same path back over the hill. I placed my own boot into the print and compared the good four inch oversize of the footprint beneath and maybe a solid two inches wider. I could picture the beast standing there staring curiously at my trail just like I was looking at his impressive tracks right now. I looked forward to seeing something besides rabbits and squirrels after the long lonely winter months in my home. My snowshoes had served me well this winter and allowed me to stay fairly active despite the depth of the snow. I would try to make a lighter less cumbersome pair this summer when I could work in the warm sunlight.

As much as I loved the snow and the trapping that I did all winter long; I still looked forward to the spring which finally came. The temperatures were mostly in the single digits throughout the winter months with an occasional thirty degrees that offered to melt some of the snow and felt like a true heat wave. When the thawing temperatures did finally come consistently, I had acclimated to the cold but was more than grateful for the sound of water dripping from the rocks and my solid little fortress. It was about three weeks after I saw the footprints when I saw my first Bigfoot walking gingerly across the opening towards the glacier. He was one of the large males that I had watched last summer with the female. He looked dusty from the knees up and clean wet black fur from the knees down as he worked his way through the two feet of snow towards the sound of running water. He looked up at me as if startled, but his face showed a faint relief as he recognized me and continued on his way. I waited for about an hour to see him coming back with his hair all wet and somewhat groomed as if he had 'cleaned up' at the glacier. I hadn't noticed any odor when I first saw him but now the familiar smell of sweat, skunk and just plain nasty filled the air and ruined the moment. Without that smell I would have just watched in awe as such an unusual sight unfolded in front of me; but the smell made me want to walk away and distance myself from the pungent odor. I had entertained the idea of following his trail to get a better idea of where he had spent the winter, but the thought of upsetting him and having to defend myself against this giant was not even an option. Besides, to follow him would mean I would have to smell his aroma again.

Two days later the large male that I had first seen at the glacier came into view, also heading for the glacier but he seemed more interested in seeing me standing by my cabin and made no effort to hide it. He was following the same path of the first male which came within fifty feet of the cabin. He was also dusty and returned from the glacier wet, black and well groomed. On his return he made his own path which led him about twenty feet from my front door and stopped for a good look at me. I was amazed at his size as he squared up with me and assessed the cabin, me and the surrounding area of my home. His face actually showed what looked like approval at what he was seeing. He spent a good bit of time looking directly at me with a curious eye but gave no indication of fear or coming any closer. I thought that I had better not smile; showing my teeth might be a sign of aggression, so I just stared back and took it all in. It was then that the smell hit me like a billowing cloud of stink as I fought to keep myself from coughing. I did however clear my throat to fight the urge which made him tighten up his posture with renewed interest. He breathed in loudly to see what his nose could tell him about this human now living in his territory, while his eyes never moved or blinked. To my surprise, he also cleared his throat as if to imitate my sound; intently looking for a reaction from me. Taking a risk I stood still and smiled at him careful not to expose my teeth. He blew out his air loudly and seemed satisfied with our interaction. After a small hesitation he turned away and headed back over the hill towards the rock slide, never looking back. Within two weeks I believe I had seen every size of these creatures possible. There were seven or eight females and an equal amount of males counting the smaller ones. There was a curiosity among the group that had them all walking close to the cabin in plain view as if to scrutinize my existence; it was fantastic to have all the company after the quiet long winter months.

As the snow melted and the warmer weather came in I was given daily viewing of the members of this family of beasts. The items around my cabin were never disturbed again after the test of my dedication to stay the prior summer. It became a common occurrence when I came home or left for fishing; I would run into one or two of them. If I was on the trail and saw them coming; I would respectfully step off the trail and let them pass within five feet of me without even a second glance from them. I started getting comfortable with the idea that this was their mountain and I had been granted permission to reside among them without any trouble. Often times I would come in from the glacier and find the younger ones milling around the cabin filling their nostrils with the smells of my man made existence.

On a beautiful clear day I decided to leave the cabin and go sit in the warm sun between my home and the area that I knew they traveled from; this would give me a better idea where their home was. That was the first time in a month that I didn't see a single one for three days; leaving me sun burnt on my face, chest and shoulders with no idea where they lived. The next couple of days was spent nursing my blistering skin and sulking about the wasted time waiting, while the entire family resumed their travels past the cabin, making plenty of noise as if to mock my attempt. I knew that sooner or later I would find out and learn a little more about their mysterious existence.

There was a feeling in the air that brought with it a new beginning of an interesting summer of coexistence, and learning each other's habits. I had never seen anything like these creatures and felt honored to be permitted to live in their element. Clearly they could have gotten me off the mountain at any time, I believe that doing me harm was not their intent at all. Their curiosity about my cabin and actions told me that they were just as intrigued with me. I began to leave my pistol at the cabin when I was not going to go very far, I knew that I would eventually have visitors from either an adult passing by or the two young males that just couldn't keep themselves from shadowing my every move. They were pretty sneaky about following me around, but often I would catch a glimpse of the red hair in the sunlight and knew they were close. They were silent;

almost too quiet for their size, I would either spot them or smell them letting me know they were near.

One day I thought I would try to see how well I could move around in the woods undetected and try to circle back on the two young males. I left the cabin as I always had and worked my way down to the creek where I did my best fishing and simply waited; sure enough I saw movement of one of my shadows cross the bank on the other side of the water. Ten feet behind the first was the second; not making a move or sound. I made plenty of noise as I always had but started looking for a path that I could slip quietly down to make my get away and circle back above their location. Directly in front of me I could see where they had chosen to hide themselves not more than sixty yards away. I have always moved up and down the side of the water as I fished and worked my way to a large tree, thick with brush all around its base. My plan was to put the tree between us and move in a straight path directly away from their location using the tree as my concealment and sound buffer. Once I knew that I was completely out of their view with the tree barrier, I slipped like a shadow backwards into the dense trees and quickly put some distance between myself and the two young males. I covered about a half mile quickly, without a single sound coming from my boots or clothes in the cool damp undergrowth. I decided that I had gone far enough and started up stream to get well ahead of my two unsuspecting followers before circling back and dropping in on their location. I stopped and knelt down to catch my breath for a second as I didn't want my breathing to become too loud. I smiled to myself to think of how expertly quiet I had been, utilizing my skills from the military I had been able to keep my breathing mostly under control. I still needed to cover the ground in a hurry before my two body guards became suspicious of my absence and started looking for me. I stood up with care not to let the branches drag on my shirt and lifted my foot to move around a truck size rock only to spot one of the young males standing on the other side twenty feet away looking right at me; even worse, the second male had walked up behind me and was standing not more than five feet away, looking at me with curiosity. Feeling like a complete idiot, I laughed out loud, actually thinking that I could have pulled it off. I smiled to myself knowing that they had never lost sight of me; sheepishly glancing at the two young males, I headed back towards the stream. Never bothering to look back, I didn't hear a single sound from my companions. The lesson that I had just been taught was that I wasn't good enough to beat them at this game; they truly were the masters of silence.

The next two months were filled with gathering fire wood and dried goods for my second upcoming winter. I realized that the two young males were going to be my constant shadow for my stay here and I had better get used to them. There were times that I would try my hand at 'shaking them' from following me but never had success. I was always up for the challenge and someday somehow I would lose them. I had collected a mountain of wood for winter heat and had made myself a stone fireplace inside the cabin close to the rear wall in hopes that the chimney and ventilation would do its job. I had also made a better set of tightly woven window shutters and built a solid door so that I could keep the wind from getting through this winter.

Feeling pretty comfortable with my cabin and its weather resistant walls I decided to build my first fire and make certain the smoke would draft upwards through the chimney. Cutting down some of my smaller pieces of wood into kindling and splitting up a few dry sections of wood I felt ready to add a little spark to the mix and enjoy the comforts of heat inside my cabin. I had about twenty boxes of wooden matches and figured that I would have to ration these out for when I didn't feel like using the flint and steel. Being the first fire in the cabin I felt it would deserve one of the matches to celebrate the occasion. After striking the match; I watched the small flame lick its way through the dry kindling and into the bigger pieces of wood. I sat back against my wooden bedframe; got comfortable and began to enjoy the mesmerizing dance of the fire as it consumed its fuel and invite a little heat into the small room. The claylike mortar that I had used in the fireplace and chimney looked to be holding up nicely as the smoke rose up the small chimney and out into the open air. As the temperature changed the smooth round river rock from cold, to hot and dry; I was startled as one of my stones cracked loudly; then seconds later two more loud pops sounded from the stone reacting to sudden temperature changes. When I say cracked I mean they broke apart as one of the halves of stone inside the chimney portion of the fireplace fell into the ventilation opening. It only took seconds before the path of smoke was blocked enough for the room to get from hazy to so full of smoke that you could not see from one end of the small cabin to the other. Rushing to the shutters I pulled them open and swung the door wide to allow the smoke to pass through.

As I rushed outside to get enough air and stop coughing, I witnessed three of the tribe members running away from my cabin area and out towards their side of the rockslide. Seconds later the large older male ran into view from the area above my cabin. The moment he saw all the smoke coming from the cabin, his expression changed drastically from concern to anger. There was no mis-understanding his facial features, my smoke signal was a threat. His direction changed to make a much larger circle around my cabin and over the rise towards the rockslide look-ing over his shoulder with a look that could not be mistaken; I had put the tribe at risk.

It was that look that told me that a fire and smoke on their mountain was the worst thing I could have brought to their home. Fire meant forest fires that carry destruc-tion or camp fires that brought unwanted hunters and campers; humans like me. The smoke had brought with it too much atten-tion for a group that wanted to remain hid-den and protected. I rushed into the cabin to pour my remaining water on the blazing fire knowing that this was the first and also the last fire I would ever have in this mountain home. I had always made my fire outdoors, close to the cabin wall in a deep spot in the ground; open fire with dry wood makes very little smoke and would have been acceptable. I made the decision to discontinue making any fire at all, I need to survive like my neighbors. I will not selfishly risk their home or existence by putting up another column of smoke.

I spent the next week removing the stones from the fireplace and closing in the wall and roof line where the chimney once protruded from the side of my building. I had not even considered whether or not to make a fire place in the cabin; for that is how civilized people lived. Realization that I would have to adapt to my surroundings and forgo a few comforts seemed a small price to pay for the privilege of being in the presence of these incredible creatures. I became heavy with guilt and sadness as the following days were alone, quiet and showed no signs of my neighbors; I had been shut out.

With the winter months closing in soon I knew that I needed to stay ahead of the cold months coming in. I would need more hides for warmth and would have to hunt for a little more food supplies to carry me through the winter. It was time to venture out for some more fish and berries. I spent six days fishing on the stream that flowed on the back of the mountainous region and not once did I see any sign of my two 'shadows'. The next two weeks were spent packing and running back and forth to the cabin with edible leaves, roots, rainbow trout and blue grouse that allowed me to get close. I can only assume that the family hunted and moved around in the darkness, or kept well-hidden over the next couple months.

It took two months before I saw one of my neighbors; I seldom heard anything in the night through those lonely months, making the silence almost unbearable. I had come out of my front door and headed up the trail towards the glacier to get some water when I felt that odd that feeling of someone watching. Not slowing my pace I scanned the trees and open area below to my right and saw nothing unusual. Looking uphill to my left I caught a glimpse of the older male standing directly in front of a large pine tree looking directly at me as if waiting for my arrival. His dark skin and brown hair blended well with the tree behind him and almost made him invisible against the colors of the tree bark. Startled at the sight, I stopped in the trail and faced him squarely; not more than twenty yards away. With my hands on my pail and feet planted firmly in the dirt I simply looked back at him with the same curiosity and felt a sense of gladness to see that I wasn't completely alone on this mountain. There was acknowledgement and apprehension in his eyes; but he showed no signs of aggression. I stood humbly with my head slightly bowed and kept my eye contact with him; this was the only way I could show my apology in hopes that he would accept.

He stood still for what felt like an eternity, staring at me like he had something heavy on his mind. With a sudden blow of his breath he took a step forward and approached my position. This certainly had my undivided attention as he continued to move towards me on the trail; should I move off the trail or should I hold still?

I stood still and remained solid in my spot thinking that with all this wide open space, if he wanted to get to the other side of me; he would just have to walk around. Then again, overthinking the situation took over, and I reached back with my foot and took a step off the trail. Out of respect; I had no position to be arrogant, it was his forgiveness that I needed. He continued to advance and I could smell his powerful stench as he was now only ten feet away. At this point I felt it best to drop my gaze and not look directly into his eyes; this might be perceived as a challenge. He walked silently across the distance and right up to me at arm's length; directly in front of me coming to a stop.

My heart was pounding so fast from adrenaline that my breath was coming quicker. His thick chest was at my eye level; the sheer mass of his frame seemed to block

Footprints of a Legend
"Elder"
Pamela McKee 2012

out the sun as he stood so close. I had no idea that he was this large as I had only seen him from a distance; I knew he was big, but this beast was simply massive. The sound of his breathing moving in and out of his huge lungs was absolutely terrifying. I turned my gaze upwards to look into his face; not too surprising that he towered over me like I was a child looking up at a parent. Standing this close and seeing into his eyes; there was a genuine kindness about them. Make no mistake about it; he was a scary fierce looking beast with a wide jawline that would take a sledge hammer hit and not even make him flinch. His high cheekbones and forehead were more like that of a human than an ape or primate. The blue eyes were piercing and curious but filled with confidence and power that should never be tested. Even from arm's length; the breath that came out with every exhale brought the most disgusting smell that made it tough not to turn away and choke out a couple of healthy coughs.

I recognized this as a pivotal moment that would determine how we would continue on our coexistence in this majestic landscape. He leaned in; inhaled deeply and kept his eyes focused on my horrified stare. Without any emotion or movement he exhaled long and loud towards my face with a low audible vocal that sounded suspiciously like 'aaaah.....' Fighting hard to keep my composure I stood still and breathed in through my mouth in an attempt to avoid the stench; but the smell was too powerful and I let out a slight cough.

He flinched slightly, but certainly not out of fear for me, or my puny little frame standing there with my little empty water pail. He turned to my right and walked a close circle around me as I stood on the side of the trail; an inspection that oddly enough felt normal. As he came back to the front of me, his large hand reached out and he felt the fabric of my shirt between his thumb and fingers. He took the pail from my hands and held it close to his face to smell it; after a close inspection, gently handed it back to me with a content look on his face. As he stepped back, he spent a fair amount of time and attention looking at my shoes. As he satisfied his curiosity about me I couldn't help but notice how physically large and heavily muscled he was. His legs were thick and built for power, but also had that long runners tone to them. Most of his bulk was throughout his chest, shoulders and arms. The top of his shoulders were thick and literally ran up into the base of his skull supporting his head with a wide neck. His forehead and top of head looked slightly coned but yet, not out of proportion. With his wide jawline and densely muscled neck and shoulders; his head and broad shoulders looked powerful and indestructible. I was absolutely terrified but actually didn't feel threatened by this magnificent male standing in front of me. Again he stepped towards me and felt the fabric on my shirt and pulled at the top button with his fingernail out of curiosity. Flicking the hard button on the soft fabric with his nail made me look down at his hand that was on my shirt. His long thick fingers and wide palm could easily cover the entire top of my head with the fingers reaching my chin. I never felt small or slight when around my peers in the military, but up against this big fella; I felt like a child. Looking at his massive hands, I could only imagine the damage he could do to me if he didn't want to be this gentle. Once he let go he stepped back about three steps letting out a bark that made me jump as the unexpected sound rang out. The bark was a word that sounded like our English word: 'Elf', but not the small cute little elf at Christmas; this was a command that was spoken with authority and meaning. He was looking up towards the tree line on the uphill side of the trail where several of the other members had appeared. I took this as an acceptance of my apology and message to the others that I was no longer a threat to their existence. He stepped forward again with his hand held high and set it down easily on the top of my head with a couple of gentle pats, barely pressing the hair down. It was the most delicate gentle touch from such a large hand, it made me thankful that he chose to forgive me and not keep me shut out. The large male then turned up the hill and disappeared into the trees with the others; for now it seemed as if everything would be back to normal.

I felt relief as the members began to show themselves over the next few weeks; I knew that I would need to win their trust again since the fire debacle. It was less lonely and made the mountain seem to come alive with the activity of our winter preparation. Periodically if I walked down the trail and a member would be coming towards me; they would simply step off to the side, only a few feet in plain view and allow me to pass. Maybe this was to have their own look at me; or possibly allow me to see them as well. I looked at this as our own corner of the earth where tradition, peace, respect and means to survive are the cohesive bond between one human and a primitive tribe.

Company of Wolves

My world has changed over the last couple of years and I was adopting an entirely new way of life with the most amazing neighbors. I felt like I was becoming part of the landscape as time rolled by but never felt completely connected with the tribe on any personal level. I know that I don't truly belong to the family and felt humbled many times by the interaction and closeness within their tight knit group. I never took for granted the company of the tribe, as the few winter months they disappeared leaving me to feel lonely, cold and desolate. I had always thought of myself as a self-sufficient man that would be alright out in the wilderness alone and not miss the company of others. Now that I have this tribe to observe and live within the same proximity; I have to say that being alone would not be something I would want long term. There were enough of them that I had to find a way to name them; start giving them identities so that I could keep track. Finding their behavior or position in the tribe would be an easy way to characterize them. The description of any one of them will always include power, strength, confidence and efficiency. I just need to be descriptive and remember them as they are now and how they change throughout the passing years. I have never gotten physically close to one since the day the massive male came close enough to touch my shirt. I was always curious to see them up close whenever we passed on the trail and was often taken back by the size of them, male and females alike. They were all very well-muscled and looked like Olympic athletes; only on a larger scale.

I had just explored a little beyond the glacier when I heard a loud cry like I have heard in the past when a member might be trying to communicate with the others. Being out and away from the rock slide, the sound was out about a half mile on the other side of the ice and down in a small clearing. This cry was different and had an almost desperate sound to it; I thought I might go and investigate as I was close. I was moving towards the open area, when the sound came once again; this time, a more frantic sound. I was much closer now as I heard thrashing and growling that I had not heard before; this could mean big trouble as I rounded the corner in the trail and saw six wolves facing off with a large female holding a young child member in her arms. She was in a poor position with a large dark male at her feet that had already lost the battle with the ferocious canines hungry for more blood. The male had been bitten and torn quite a few times, and there were three lifeless wolves scattered on the ground in front of them. With all the loose hair on the ground and in the area, I can only imagine the battle that had been fought prior to my arrival. The female had her back to a corner in the rocks that provided no escape; and the adult male member with the three had been taken out already; the next few moments did not look good for the female and her child. I had never seen her before and this was the first time I had seen a child this small for that matter; they were not native to this tribe.

The smell of blood only fueled the excitement of the wolf pack as they took turns reaching in and snapping at the female who swung blindly at them with a sturdy looking branch in her hand. Her eyes were wide with fear as the whites of her eyes gave her a wild, crazed appearance. She had bright blue eyes, similar to the older male that I had encountered on several occasions; this had to be one of his offspring. Not even thinking that I was out in the open with no cover; I shouted loudly, "Hey, get out of there!" This didn't really seem to scare the wolves at all; more accurately it distracted the female. As she looked at me in horror the wolves lunged in at the opportunity and got a hold of her arm that held the branch. The violence in which the wolves lunged at her made her grip on the child fail and the youth dropped to the ground at her feet. With her other arm free she stepped over the child, planting a foot on either side of the youngster and squatted down over the little one grabbing at the wolf on her arm. Baring her teeth, she sank them deep into the back of the neck of the animal and tore away at the flesh, but the others were closing in quickly. All of this played out in two or three seconds as I reached for my pistol and fired into the air. 'Five shots left,' I thought to myself as I lowered the muzzle towards one of the vicious attackers. The shot had startled them all, but I knew by the way they stood their ground that I had no other choice. My next shot landed true and dropped the wolf she had hold of; the following shot did not seem to affect the second wolf as he lunged at the female's neck with his sharp teeth. He got a hold on her and violently shook his head from side to side pulling away a thick piece of flesh from the side of her neck. He lunged in again for another hold but my additional shot finished the job, as the impact threw him to the side. All the while, I am advancing on the horrific scene with awkward steps across the uneven trail. I shot again but missed all together as I lined up for my sixth shot and wounded the wolf closest to the female who lunged. 'Zero bullets left' I mumbled aloud as I watched the remaining pack turn and run into the wood line with their awkward sideways gate.

That was a very close call as I stopped in the trail and looked down at my weapon; this was the second time I had fired the .45 since I had left civilization. My attention turned to the sound of several running footsteps advancing up the trail from behind me. I looked back down to see the female crouched down, clinging to her child with her good arm and bleeding profusely from the wound on the side of her neck. She looked up at me in horror as she reached with her bad arm for the branch that she had dropped. She was down on her knee with her hips against her fallen male companion; the look in her eyes was that of: 'I will fight for you until the last ounce of blood leaves my veins'.

She looked past me on the trail at the approaching sound of footsteps. Coming down the trail were four of the tribe members that I had seen in the past; I stood up and backed away. Like an emergency crew they ran past me within inches as if I did not exist and gathered up the deceased male, helped the female to her feet, taking the young one from her arms. The fourth member looked closely at the wolves but did not attempt to take or move them from where they had fallen. There seemed to be a little focus as to how they died and how I had come to be there with the three unfamiliar members. As if I were invisible; they moved quickly from the area where the horrible scene had played out. Still running they headed for the rock slide; never once looking back.

I stood in the middle of the trail; once again alone, holding an empty gun wondering how this could have happened. Everything had happened so fast; had the use of the gun put me at odds with the tribe once again? This was the second time that I had fired my weapon since I had left Missoula Montana; I had a feeling that this weapon was destined to bring trouble forever. I drew six more rounds from my pocket and reloaded the weapon and slid it back in its holster. It would be difficult to explain the reasoning behind the use of such a loud firearm and the attention that it might bring to this mountain. I turned back up the trail carefully watching the tree line where the wolves had gone and headed for my cabin. I think that my actions will have some kind of consequences but given the situation, I had to intervene rather than let it play out where it was headed. With heavy heart and weary steps I made my way back to the cabin and found the familiar two young males in front to the doorway waiting.

"Howdy boys, been waiting long?" I asked out loud, feeling I had little to lose at this point.

I didn't have to be told out loud that they were there to see me; but the question was: How much trouble was I in? They both stepped quietly aside as I approached, the expressions had changed on their faces when they heard my voice; I'm guessing it threw them off a bit. They allowed me to enter the doorway to my cabin without any problem; once inside they stood post outside as if to make sure I didn't leave. I stood in the doorway and looked at the backs of the two young males who appeared to be standing guard on my home. They weren't budging and I certainly wasn't pushing; it just felt like jail for the night. The thought of dropping out my window crossed my mind, but my better judgement kept me where I was. I attempted to lie down and rest but the concern of what the following day would bring had me feeling uneasy. I must have fallen asleep eventually as a thump on the wall of my cabin startled me into the upright position on my homemade wooden bed.

Baby Blues and a Funeral

It was daylight and still quite early in the morning; but I was wide awake. My two guards were standing outside looking in; waiting for me to come to the doorway. I brought my feet off the end of the bed and stood up slowly hoping the upcoming moments outside would not be too difficult. I stepped out into the open air to see several more of the tribe members standing around in a half circle near the entrance of the cabin;

this didn't look good at all. The two young males came in behind me and the several members started moving towards the rock slide area as if herding me towards their side of the hill. I had no idea what I was about to get into but at this point in the game, with the company I was keeping, the thought of having a choice didn't even come to mind. We moved in silence as we moved along the hillside towards the massive rock slide with an occasional sideways glance from the members as we walked.

Reaching the rocks was quicker as we all had formed a line and I followed a tall older female who looked to be frowning. She had the similar features as the others with the strong lines of power and solid muscle mass; but her face was tired with very pronounced frown lines though the brow. As a female she had a slightly smaller frame than the males but her arms and calves made up for everything she lacked in height. I mention her arms and forearms because they were actually larger than the male who was taller and heavier. Her eyes looked tired but she had a mean look; enough to rip your arm off and beat you with it. She had very yellow teeth with a crooked mouth like that of someone who had maybe suffered a stroke. The members all worked their way navigating around the tricky rock formations, but she walked with smooth precision and a flawless flow that made everyone look clumsy by comparison. We dropped into a low point in the rocks where I was able to see an overhanging rock with an empty void under it. The flat rock beneath the overhang was large and flat with a fairly steep grade that sloped into the opening. The flat surface was dirty and was the only visible sign that there was any kind of traffic in or out of the opening. This was the point of entry to a cave that couldn't be seen until you were directly on top of it. Looking around I noticed that you had to be within ten or twelve feet of the entrance to even be able to find it, the concealment to this opening was incredible. It was a huge rockslide that ran up the side of the mountain maybe a thousand yards and downwards maybe the same distance. If I had to guess

I would put it at a half mile wide. How on earth could they have a cave in the middle of this slide, or how could they have found it for that matter?

This is where it got interesting as my two guards stepped forward on each side of the entryway; as if making certain that I didn't miss the mark of where I was supposed to go in. The smell coming from inside was horrendous as the breeze came from inside and made me nauseous. I found myself grazing my hands on the side of the walls as I entered the dark cool entry. The doorway of the cave was low enough that I had to duck my head to get through but was able to stand upright within the first three feet. The feeling of going directly into a trap was playing out in my mind as I stepped into the darkness. There was a light source from above to the far left in the open room that gave enough light to make my way inside without falling on my face. I was able to see several yards into the cave, but the smell and the feeling of being confined was almost too much for my mind as the two 'guards' came in behind me, closing off any chance of escape. With the opening about six feet behind me I was able to see that the space opened up into a fairly large room; in fact it was plenty large with a high ceiling and wide, similar to a spacious living area in a large house. There were several other members in the open room; one of which was the adult female with her small child. She was sitting against the solid stone wall to my left and did not look very lively as I'm sure her injuries from the previous day had taken its toll. The youngster was sitting beside her with its arms tightly wrapped around the waist of its mother. The small face was turned away from me as it continued to 'nestle' into the side of her last living parent. I was adjusting to the darkness and was able to see a little more clearly throughout the room. The adult females forearm and hand looked a mess as the wolves had torn away quite a bit of flesh in those few short seconds. Her neck was still showing fresh blood and she was black with dried blood that covered the entire side of her body; the fact that she was still alive was incredible.

With this amount of blood loss and the shallow sounds of her breathing told me that her time was limited. Standing just a few feet away; the large male whom I recognized as their leader, was standing over her. There was another female close beside him as they both looked up at me. I had no idea why I was in this room with them but somehow the female and small child were part of the equation. The two males behind me separated with one standing fixed at the entrance and the second brushing past me and into an opening that led off to the right and out of sight. As he passed I saw the red color to his hair and understood that he still wasn't fond of me and the one still behind me was the one that I had cut.

There was an opening that split off out of the room to the left that you could hear a loud steady drip of water. But from the opening to the right I could hear what sounded like a fast running stream in the distance. The sound of the water was periodically blocked off as the male made his way down the path, putting his dense body between my position and the sound of the running water. I figure he had gone a good fifty or sixty yards away before the sound was clear and steady; making the running water just over fifty yards away from where I stood, in my estimation. Having full time running water explained how they could stay hidden inside this cave as long as they had stored enough food to stay fed through those winter months. This was a lot of information to take in all at once, but I was completely puzzled still, as to why I was standing inside this cave with them right now. The smell was pungent and the room was cool and damp with a slight steady breeze moving through the room which didn't help the heavy odor surrounding me. I stood still and waited for the large male and female to make up their minds as to what to do with me. My eyes were fully adjusted to the lighting in the room and details were much better now.

The small child that was clinging to the female pulled away from the female again and turned to look at me; even in the dimly lit room, it was her brilliant blue eyes that caught my attention the most. She was different in her own way as even her facial features were more human and less hairy than all the rest. The little one didn't even appear upset or afraid of her surroundings and blinked curiously at me in the dark room. I knew there had to be a connection between the large male, the wounded female, and the small female youth at their feet. The blues eyes were the same brilliant blue color and stood out from the dark features of their faces.

Suddenly the large female let out a gasp as the little girl broke away and scrambled over to where I stood. She stood on her two feet awkwardly and wrapped her arms around my leg and looked up at me with those brilliant blue eyes without any fear or hesitation. I was startled by the situation and was surprised with the feeling of actually being touched by someone. Contact like this had not happened in such a long time that it was almost intrusive; until I looked into those innocent blue eyes and my heart melted. She was not going to take no for an answer as she started making an effort to climb…

The two adults standing by were puzzled by this action and stood still as if they were also unsure as how to handle this situation. Instinctively I reached down to help the infant up as it appeared that she wanted to be held; like any child would. It seemed natural to pick her up and place her on my hip and have her wrap her little arms around my neck for support. This was exactly what she wanted as she burrowed her face into my chest and remained still. I was lost at this point; I had no idea what to do next as the mother made her way to her knees and made an attempt to come over to where I stood. Taking this as my cue I moved over to where she was and knelt down in front of her to hand off the baby. She made no effort to take the child; the wounded mother simply stroked her good hand gently across the little ones back. I stayed there kneeling on the hard dark surface waiting patiently as the little baby clung to my neck and its mother tried to soothe her little baby girl.

I'm sure she struggled with her own mixed feelings about the child's sudden interest in the human. The mother looked intently at me with anguish, curiosity and hope, as she knew her life was fading. I didn't want to be here in this situation; I didn't ask for this little child to choose me for comfort when there were so many other family members around.

I certainly did not want to look back up at those two adults who hadn't moved an inch once I had entered the cave. I didn't have to; the adult male walked up behind me and gently pulled me to my feet. Still holding the young girl I turned and faced him completely baffled as to why they had brought me here in the first place. The female, still kneeling at our feet reached out for my hand and looked at me with her dark tired eyes and pulled my hand to her face as if to say thank you for everything you have done. She was big; her hands were much larger than mine but her touch was as gentle as I have ever felt. Her hands trembled but there was no mistaking her genuine feeling of appreciation. It was at this point that the other large female came up beside us and opened her hands in a gesture to hand her the baby; which I was glad to do. The little girl held on for a brief moment; long enough to look into my eyes with her big blue eyes. Her face had very little hair like the others, her jaw was wide but her forehead and skull features were what I would perceive as a normal human child. Even at her youthful age, the physical structure of her body was that of strength and tone. Her crystal blue eyes were lively and bright as she curiously looked into my face; she was connecting with me in her own way. I had a feeling I would be seeing this one around quite a bit from now on.

With the birthmother having made her statement; she settled heavily back against the wall as an exhausted sigh escaped her lips. The other female walked silently away into the depth on the right side path of the cave. The adult male pulled me to my feet escorted me towards the entrance of the cave. The guard stepped aside allowing us to proceed to the opening I had been long-ing for. I leaned forward emerging out of the cave and into the light taking a deep breath of the fresh air I had been deprived of.

Back out in the open air, I was astonished (with) how pure the outside air tasted and how wonderful it was to feel the beautiful sun shining on my face again. I had been inside that cave for maybe fifteen minutes; with each tedious minute weighting like they could be your last, it felt like a lifetime had passed. I turned around to see what was expected of me only to find myself standing alone at the entrance. No one was in sight; not even the guard followed me out. It felt odd, but the relief of being free from the confinement was welcoming.

I made my way back to my cabin and lay down on my bed; my head was reeling with excitement and wonder. Several hours into the night, I heard a series of long howls from the rock-slide area. They emerged from on the other side of the rocks and the sounds were filled with a deep and heavy sorrow.

It was a lonely sound like that of a wolf, but with volume and length; the howl was reflected something much more different and heart wrenching. Over my time here on the mountain, I have heard these howls previously; but tonight the sound didn't invoke fear, but filled me with a feeling of sadness and empathy. This was the sound of raw pain, sorrow and loss; this sound was meant to express that of mourning a loved one who was gone forever.

Funeral for a Mother

I felt like I was the only living creature on this mountain over the next two days; it was as if the earth had stopped. I did not see or hear from the tribe, who I know resided within the cave. From my guess, they could remain inside the cave for weeks or maybe even months, never emerging out into the light until their food supply had run out. I felt a bit of abandonment as the second day came to a close and the sun was setting low in the western horizon.

The calm and silence was shattered by the sound of a howl and scream combination; the kind of scream I had heard in the past from the tribe members. Only this evening it was a duet; it was two voices in unison as the scream sliced into the evening calm with its soulful, sad, and heartbroken sounds. With the shadows arising across the mountain and the darkness closing in, the howl cast a heavy blanket of gloom across the valley. The volume of the song was powerful and gripped the air with one voice dropping off and then slowly starting again before the second had finished. It was a continuous melody bringing chills to every inch of my body. Approximately ten minutes of these soulful cries danced off the mountain tops; then without warning everything collapsed into an eerie silence. There was not a single sound; not even birds, squirrels, wind or a single insect. The universe stopped to pay its respect for the pain of the tribe. I came to the conclusion that the female who battled the wolves had finally succumbed to her injuries. The sounds of their agony in letting her go as the family members felt deep loss. It was truly sobering but the respect and anguish that was projected was incredible. I was just taking my first step back into the cabin when the young male, with the scar on his face, showed up beside me without a sound. His appearance out of thin air startled me and I jumped backwards hitting the door with a loud thud. The noise caused him to tense up in a defensive position and we both froze for a moment taking quick inventory of the current situation and gauging the level of threat to ensure that it would not get out of hand. We both realized that it was my reaction that started the tension and the mood soon lightened up enough for him to turn his posture to the side cueing for me to follow. This would be the second time that I had been invited to follow him and possibly get another glimpse into their mysterious lives. I obliged and followed without a sound as we made our way back through the rocks to the cave entrance. Only this time, we did not stop at the entrance but continued beyond to the other side of the rock-slide.

It was dusk, but the clear sky and three quarter moon was bright, casting enough light for us to see perfectly. As we rose over the slight ridge-line, I counted eleven adult tribe members and one little child being held by the frowning adult female. They were all standing in the grass at the bottom of the slide area. The older male and female were separated from the group and standing on a flat rock slightly elevated above the others as if prepared to give a presentation. Many of the tribe members showed no interest in my presence but a couple displayed a bit of aggression towards the newcomer being present. The frowning female made her way down to me and pulled on my shirt signaling me to follow her to a vantage point closer to where the older couple stood elevated. There was no mistaking the little ones desire to be passed off to me; this made no sense to me, but I welcomed the small female into my arms as she reached towards me without hesitation. She immediately wrapped her legs around my waist and clung to my neck with no sign of letting go. She leaned away looking into my face as if to examine me intently, then leaned back in and rested her head on my chest and neck. Without knowing who I was or what I was, this little girl was fearless and was beginning to win me over.

I was so engrossed in the process of the female handing me the child and our interaction, before I finally got a moment to see what else was taking place. Everyone was standing still giving the couple who stood above them their complete undivided attention. Not a sound was made, and everyone stood perfectly still as two members from the cave came over the ridge-line carrying the female who had been left to fight the wolves. She was held with the utmost respect and care as they picked their way down to the others. She was laid down tenderly on a flat surface and the group methodically proceeded to pick up rocks from the rock-slide and placed them out in the grass beyond the bottom of the slide. This is when the second duet began; the large male and female standing above began their soulful song presenting their memorial. I watched in amazement as they worked tirelessly and efficiently removing stones; one after another. The stones were placed carefully on the grass at the furthest point of the lush clearing, meticulously placed in order as they worked their way through the void. They seemed to never get in the way of each other but excavated the area quickly with clean precision. The song continue on for about five minutes and then faded as the couple stood now silent as the stones were removed. The only sounds were of an occasional rock sliding against the rough surface of another, and a periodic loud exhale from the workers. In silence they continued like army ants on a mission, as the time passed by. Within three hours there was a wide path back into the slide cascading all the way down, reaching the dirt. It was six to eight feet wide and advanced back close to twenty feet getting deeper as they progressed. As they reached beyond the twenty foot mark I began to see the remains of bones and skulls from others who had previously passed away over the years. This was a long time to stand with a small child hanging on your neck, so I eventually sat down on the flat surface and positioned the young female on my lap who ultimately ended up laying on the surface beside me with her head on my lap sleeping soundly. The contact was welcome as it had been forever since I have had any kind of interaction.

Today was a funeral unlike anything I ever witnessed; this was respect and family loyalty at its finest. The opening was clean and the path was clear of anything with the remains of the deceased at the end of the excavation. The members all stood in two separate rows on each side of the opening and left the center aisle open. It was now that the older couple left their elevated position and arrived at the entrance of the fresh dirt path. Together they picked up the female and proceeded to the inside of the opening; carrying their loved one to her final resting place. They passed by slowly, every tribal member reached forward in silence and gently touched the face and head of the female as she was carried by. Once at the end, they placed her gingerly on the surface of the ground beside the other remains and stood over her. The male placed his arm over the female's shoulders and they faced each other imparting a strong embrace. In unison, they both leaned down to touch the face of the female and turned leaving the open space. Meanwhile the rest of the members had stood like stone statues and waited respectfully. The couple now walked out into the open grass, each picking up a stone and brought them into the opening delicately placing them on top of the female. This began the refilling process where every tribe member began to fill in the entire opening. This took roughly two hours as they all worked in harmony replacing the rock-slide back to its original form. When the slide was completely filled; not one single stone remained in the grass below the slide. This mountain would always hide the evidence of the tribe that relied on its secret existence. The couple again took their position on the flat stone as the others moved by in single file; with the last one being the frowning female who then opened her arms, taking the young girl from beside me. There was an awkward hesitation before the young female allowed the adult female to take her away, but eventually chose to reach out and embraced the idea. It was an interesting feeling, I almost didn't want to give her back; I had found comfort in the companionship with another living soul. This little one had gotten to me with her innocent face and immediate trust of this human within the sacred house of the tribe.

The next couple of weeks were filled with life changing and lasting events that would influence my way of life as long as I continued my life on this beautiful mountain. I was 'gifted' with a house guest the very next day.

I was prepared to leave on a three or four day hunting trip; as I closed the door and turned to leave, I ran directly into three guests One was the old frowning adult female, the young male with a scar on his face and lastly the adorable little blue eyed bundle of energy. Now don't get me wrong; I love having company, but the amount of energy that this little three foot blue eyed girl possessed was going to test my own stamina levels. The frowning adult female literally placed the young girl right in my path, stepped backwards a few steps, and waited to see what I would do next. Meanwhile the little blue eyed girl worked her way towards me and clung to my pant leg and began to pull; looking up at me with those bright eyes full of mischief. She almost had a smile on her face but for the most part her facial and body expressions were dry and aloof; it was the eyes that did all her communicating. Why in the heck would they bring this little girl to me when there were clearly so many suitable family members in the tribe to care for her? This new adventure was going to test my patience and force me in my ability to communicate with the tribe. Maybe that was the whole idea; include and involve me with her upbringing and opening the door of communication between myself and the tribe.

It was a genius plan, but not what I signed up for when I came out here in the mountains. This would hinder my hunting and fishing in my summer months, especially when it was so vital for me to gather supplies in preparation for the cold winter months ahead. I would go along with this for now and attempt to manage this new task, but first I needed to find a way to break away and take care of my own responsibilities. I would start by spending a lot of time picking berries, gathering leaves and looking for items that I could use, in the immediate area.

I must admit, the company was welcome and I found myself smiling and speaking softly to the little one who I decided to name 'Little Blue'. She was surprisingly agile and could more or less keep up with my pace of walking as I scoured the terrain through the brush and trees. Never, did I have to wonder where the frowning adult was; she was the most amazing shadow who made no secret of her presence. The young male only showed up every few days as the weeks went by; he only hung around for about an hour, then disappeared without a sound. Little Blue didn't come to the cabin every day; but I would say easily, four or five days a week as the summer raced by. Every morning when 'Mrs. Frowny' brought Little Blue to the cabin I would greet them; "Good morning Little Blue," and with a nod, "Mrs. Frowny" then I would gesture towards myself and finish with "John Stone." In the evening when the sun started dipping towards the western mountains, the adult female, whom I named 'Mrs. Frowny', would stand up from wherever she was and simply take Little Blues hand and walk towards the rock slide. I must say that the time was well spent and realistically, Mrs. Frowny was as much tasked with the new babysitting responsibility as I was.

The summer turned quickly into fall and the big freeze followed in no time. Little Blue would be kept in the cave for the winter and I was left to my own devices to gather as much fish and supplies as I could before the first big snow hit. I felt the loneliness creeping back in as the weeks went by without company; and I had to get prepared for the unforgiving months ahead. My supplies were lean and the hopes of getting a hunt in before the snow hit was pretty slim, so it was all about how much fish I could catch and what I could tempt into my traps. My snow shoes were ready, but I really wanted the option of being able to stay put in the cabin if I chose.

I was coming back to the cabin late from one of my chilly fall fishing trips where the 'catch of the day' had eluded my lure hiding in the depths of the perfect fishing hole. Feeling defeated and tired from all the distance that I had covered, I made my way through the trees toward my home amongst the trail surrounded by darkness. When you travel the same path for months on end you don't always need the sun or clear moonlight to light your way; you simply know the path home. I was not more than fifteen feet from my front door when I tripped over something big lying in the middle of the path. With a sad string of three fish in one hand and small fishing pole in the other, I hit the ground hard; hurling into the dirt as the object in my path came up to my knees.

I remember falling forward but the crushing blow to my face against the hard packed earth was enough to rob me of my consciousness and put a nice long split on my chin. When I was able to gather my wits, I pulled my hands up under my chest and pushed myself up off the ground however my shins and feet were resting on something still in the trail. As I pushed off, the obstacle felt funny and rolled slightly with my weight. It was unnatural, and frightened me to the point where I crawled on my hands and knees about six feet away; leapt to my feet and ran to the door of my cabin. Swinging the door open, I felt aggravated that my space was being infringed on. There was something out there, and I had no clue what was on that trail, but I needed to know.

I stood in the doorway for about two full minutes straining my eyes in the darkness; there was an outline of something on the trail but I couldn't quite make out what is could be. I took a long stick from the side of the doorway and held it out in front of me and cautiously approached the dark shadow in the trail. It was one of those nights where the overcast clouds didn't allow any light, let alone a sliver from the moon and being able to see in the dark was almost impossible. The stick bumped the object; I pushed hard and it moved slightly. It rolled a little but was very heavy; it was not solid and hard like a rock or log, this had a soft surface that gave to pressure. The surface felt like fur which indicated something that had fallen on the trail. There was no skunk like stench that was always present with the tribe, but the smell of elk was more what I was detecting. Still holding the stick, I made my way closer to the object and reached out to find thick hair of an animal in the trail. To my relief, it was the body of an elk; a small yearling that had somehow found its way to my cabin. I felt along the outside of the elk to get a better idea of its size and weight when I felt something beside it. There were also six rabbits laying beside the carcass.

These had been placed here on purpose; the tribe had provided me with a bounty from their hunt. It was as if they knew the time I spent this summer with Little Blue was time I needed to get supplies. This was more than enough to get me through; this was truly, a life saver. I went to work skinning and preparing the elk in the darkness. The rabbits were quick and easy to skin and prepare but the elk was the real prize. The fur from this elk would be perfect to keep off the cold this winter. I truly owed a huge debt to my neighbors. I worked through the next few hours and hung everything out to dry; with this much food on hand, I could settle into the winter months without concern of making it through. Exhausted, I cleaned up and went to bed thinking about the generous gift that I had received; even in the wild back country of Montana; neighbors looked out for each other.

Diary of a Tripwire

I decided that it was time to capture all of this life and write a diary of the activities and prepare someone for what they might stumble into if they ever wandered this deep into the wilderness. It brings me comfort to know that even if no one ever reads my words; it's still here as a record of my own life, as I will not share this with another human. I have never been much of a writer, but I take pride in remembering what mysteries and amazing findings are available to me every day. A diary is a very personal journey that digs deep into the emotion and soul of the writer who truly opens up for the pages, and this will be my masterpiece. I didn't know why I brought this journal out in the woods in the first place, until I realized that so much was taking place so fast. There are memories I don't want to forget, so I write them down, that way they won't slip away with the years.

I had always carried my gun out in the mountains and have not fired off a shot since the wolves attacked that family; putting it away was just one of those sacrifice's I would have to make. I turned the pistol away towards the floor and released the cylinder, I slowly pulled the six bullets out. It was time to retire the gun and store it away; it was simply a weight I didn't need to carry. I wrapped the heavy nickel plated weapon in an oil cloth and put the bullets in a pouch with my father's picture. I hung the pouch up high on the center beam of the cabin, close enough so I could always see them to remind me where they were, but far enough to keep me from relying on the weapon. Storing the .45 and the rounds in separate places would ensure that it could never be used by curious fingers that may find their way into the cabin in my absence. There was a feeling of surrender when putting it away; anything outside those walls would just have to be negotiated without a firearm.

I spent the winter in solitude, and anxiously awaited the arrival of summer so I could once again see my neighbors and feel less secluded. It was when the ground became exposed that I started seeing the tribe again. The first couple of weeks showed only a few members emerge as they made their way to the water for the yearly bath. It was good to see movement after the long quiet months, and not one went by without intensely watching towards the cabin. I sensed that they had missed seeing me too through the cold months, or they were curious to see if I made it through a bad winter. Then the sightings stopped; six days without a sight, sound, track, or smell.

Finally, early one morning I heard the single howl of the sorrowful cry of what I now recognized as loss; the same sound that lingers and embodies the pain of a fallen loved one. Curious, I made my way to the other side of the rock-slide keeping a good distance away to observe, but not to intrude. The procession had already been well under way as all the stones had been removed and all the tribe members were standing by. This time there were two adult males who brought a completely silver male member out, into the slide area. I had never seen this; all silver, male before in my couple years of being with this tribe. I can only guess that he had always stayed confined to the cave as his body was thin and fragile, the signs of age and arthritis in his hands and joints were apparent. This was a passing that I am sure they were all anticipating. Every tribal member was able to reach out and touch the face and head of the deceased as he was carried by; again displaying pure respect and honor. I saw Little Blue standing within the ranks of tribal members, and was shocked at how much she had grown through the winter months. She was a bit taller for sure, it was defiantly more growth than we, as humans grow. Her body was filling out with more muscular definition and her face was transforming as well. She still had very little hair on her face, but her eyes stood out like brilliant color in a black and white photo. She looked up at my position with what appeared to be a gleam in her eyes; it was one of recognition, the same way you would look at a good friend you hadn't seen in forever.

As the two males settled the silver elder in his final resting place, the entire tribe knelt down in the freshly exposed dirt. As they leaned forward from the kneeling position, they all pounded their fists into the soil in front of them. The rhythm was slow at first but increased with speed and impact to a good sixty second beat, then faded to silence as they all sat back on their heels, facing each other. From my position, the sound rose up from the ground like thundering hooves of wild horses running by. It was amazing to see their culture as they buried someone who was very old and clearly held a great position among the tribe. The display of tribal respect and conduct in dealing with the loss was different than the other funeral that I had witnessed; this was similar in burial but held a much different in ritual. One by one, the members stood up from the deepest part of the trench to the front and they stood silently with heads down for about five minutes. The tribe began the methodic replacement of the stones into the rock-slide, this was my moment to retreat back to my home for a little cabin cleaning for the day.

The summer was busy with my new shadow, Little Blue by my side, picking berries with some occasional fishing on the side. Every morning the greeting, "Good morning Little Blue" was the best way I could start my day. The first month with the tribe consisted of Little Blue and Mrs. Frowny in the background shadowing everything I did. I don't believe Mrs. Frowny was as entertained by my early morning greetings as Little Blue and I; but it would continue, simply because her lack of interaction made it that much more amusing to me. I would always speak to Little Blue with the idea that someday she would understand what I was trying to communicate. Always pointing to myself and saying "John Stone" was the only way to get her to understand my identity. I would also point out items and tell her the names of them but she always beamed when I would gesture towards her and say "Little Blue." She was maturing fast and was easily able to keep up with my pace in the woods; I feared she would be able to outrun me by the next summer as rapidly as she was growing. Humans take quite a bit of time to grow; but I watched in amazement as she literally grew by leaps and bounds; I am guessing that with her genetics she would reach full mature size in the next couple years. I enjoyed her company and was delighted in the time I was able to spend with the tribe. As an outsider I was at the point that I could walk among them without even a second glance as they went about their business. The comfort level was finally at a point where Little Blue would show up without her unhappy escort, and the tribe would not even bother to come looking for her. She was an excellent running partner in the woods; she had a great nose and ear for things I could not hear or smell. We soon became an efficient hunting team and were able to play off of each other's strengths to navigate the wilderness with the best of them. We often came back with more rabbits than the other members of the tribe. I don't believe they took the time to count how many we had and compare their numbers against ours, but I enjoyed my own competitive nature when it came to hunting. I also understood that without Little Blue's help; my own numbers would decrease significantly.

One warm summer day I decided to just be lazy and hang around the hillside below the rock slide where a group of members were sunning and picking through the remaining berries that had not been scavenged. Several of the tribe had wondered off to the lower side of the large meadow into a medium size grove of trees that offered some shade from the hot mid-day sun. They were quiet and seemed not to have a care in the world as they scratched at the ground searching for grubs, rodents and tender green leaves to chew on. One of the females had stumbled upon a small nest of bees under the base of a fallen tree and was waving off the pesky insects as she tried to get to the sweet honey combs just inches below the rotting wood. I stayed a good distance away so as not to encroach on her feeding area, let alone catch the attention of the irritated bees. To her right a large older male, not more than ten feet away stood up straight and swatted at one of the insects that started buzzing around his face. Satisfied that he had ended the intruding little pest, he turned away with a renewed interest in the sweet ripe berries at his feet. The quick motion of the male might have drawn the attention of the bees or he was just in the wrong place at the wrong time, but one of the flying tormentors made his way through the tall grass and hit the male in the left eye. The male jumped sideways, clearly irritated by the bee that had just stung him in the corner of the eye. It didn't seem odd at the time watching this large 400 pound male react to such a small insignificant insect, but the outcome was memorable.

Any size creature will flinch or shy away from the little stinger baring insects as they pose an uncomfortable sensation that is more than irritating. The left eye immediately began to swell; the following sixty seconds forced the eye completely closed. Two more minutes and his nose and cheek began to take on fluid and round out his face in an odd contortion. Shaking his head violently his breathing became loud and hoarse. The reaction from the sting was surprising as well as unexpected; you don't think of animals being allergic to bees and having anaphylactic shock. The distressed male dropped to his knees and began to choke against the pressure growing on the side of his face and swelling in his neck and throat. He was wiping his hands across the left side of his face as if to brush away whatever it was that was smothering him, but the swelling was happening so rapidly that his throat was pinching off his air.

A smaller male and adult female showed a little interest, but seemed unaffected as to what was happening. I'm sure they couldn't understand the seriousness of what was playing out right in front of them. Now, laying on the ground and kicking frantically into the grass, his hoarse breath coughed out a few more passes as he fought to draw in more air. There was a small whistle of air that pulled in, but not enough to fuel the body with the necessary amount of oxygen. His legs kicked out straight, and he tensed up every muscle in a last effort to pull in one more desperate breath; he relaxed and his body went limp. I watched in amazement as the entire incident took no more than seven minutes from the initial sting to the last breath of air passing through the adult male's lungs. With his breathing stopped and his thrashing movements now quiet the male lay lifeless on the ground. The female that was close came up to him to investigate all the noise followed by silence and reached out for his hand. Her face showed true horror as the realization that the male was dead. The female let out a small primal scream of distress that was short, but very effective. The reaction of the adult female started to draw a little more attention from the rest of the group; one by one, they began to realize that the male was just simply dead without knowing why. For a tribe such as this, I was surprised to see how much emotion and visible pain that each one felt when they lost a member.

I stepped back as one of the larger males and female came in hoisting the deceased onto the shoulders of a third male and walked away towards their home. The rest of the tribe dropped into silence emoting sadness while falling into procession on the trail behind the fallen male; more of a strange forced procession. Once back at the cave the ritual of removing stones began as the void in the rock-slide opened up once again to consume and hide in its depths another tribe member. Even though I witnessed two of these burials; I knew I was not considered part of the family and would not be allowed to help. This was difficult and I had to restrain as I really wanted to show my respects and participate.

The young red colored male was more affected by the funeral than the rest of them as he watched from the flat stone platform above the slide and carried an infinite pain in his eyes. He never stood still through the entire event as he shifted from side to side with anxiety, the sun danced through the red colored hair that covered his body. He leapt from his lofty position as they set the male down in his final resting place. Moving with haste he entered the opening towards the dead male and paused walking up with the hesitation of someone who didn't want to believe. Dropping to his knees in front of the body he laid his head on the chest of the older male that I guessed to be his father. Coming in behind him stood his best friend, with the long running scar on his face, and dropped down draping his arm over the broad shoulders of his companion. It was a heartfelt display of agonizing loss for this young male; it was on this day that he would assume the duties as a tribe provider and hunter. Standing up, he looked back at the tribe with sadness and distress as he pushed out his pain with a howl of agony that cut through the quiet afternoon air. He stood absolutely still with his head hung low and eyes closed for about ten minutes; the tribe also stood frozen in time as they waited respectfully for this young member to absorb the tragedy and allow the covering to begin. Opening his eyes and raising his gaze throughout his fellow tribe members, he returned to his position with a much different posture; one of pride and preparedness to take on his new more difficult role.

I made my way back to the cabin to rest and reflect upon the day's events with the loss of another tribe member. I had been with this family for three years now and was always impressed at their customs and unwavering respect for one another; I smiled and drifted off to sleep as the cool afternoon brought the nighttime darkness. The next few months flew by with gathering food and provisions for my cabin and whatever I could contribute to the tribe as far as assisting with quartering their elk or deer for storing in the deep crevices of the glacier. I was beginning to feel like one of the family; hunting alongside some of the greatest creatures on the planet, it was one of my greatest honors.

I was accompanied by Little Blue throughout the entire summer and fall; we were able to communicate with facial expressions and basic hand gestures. I always would speak single words with items that I hoped she would understand; but for now she would look, listen and show her understanding with her expressive eyes. I was starting to build a tremendous friendship with an up and coming female tribal warrior. She had grown through the summer, physically as a young adult and tactically as a hunter. This tribe of mysterious creatures was now my family, and I was certainly becoming a member of their tribe.

1979 Night in the Day

I had now been in the mountains with the tribe for six years and always been allowed to run freely with the family as one of their own for the last three years. I had come to understand their culture and behaviors fairly well over that short period of time. Every day was all about gathering food for the young and elderly who rarely left the cave, and the amount of food consumed by the tribe was quite staggering. They did not hibernate and sleep off the winter months like a bear, but fed freely throughout the entire year. Their winter months were pretty much confined to the cave as the deep snow only allowed the strongest to venture out for cold weather hunting. I was allowed to sometimes tag along with my snowshoes which made it possible to keep up as they had to forge through the chest high drifts and steep inclines. With my best efforts to keep track of months and years, it was mid-February in the year 1979 when I noticed an odd shift in the behavior of the tribe for a few weeks. Even in the middle of the heavy weather, several of the larger members of the tribe began pushing the snow away from the front of the entrance and opening a wide trail out into the lower clearing. Using their hands to scoop the snow away, they worked continuously to create a large opening just below the rocks into the grassy area below. Their work opened up a sizeable space that went all the way down to the ground below, which made easy access for all the members to come out in the open air. I did not spend time in the cave, so I cannot be sure if this was due to something inside that they needed to get away from. It could be they felt an early spring coming and were getting prepared for freedom away from the confines of the stone walls. I had seen them begin clearing the snow each year but not until May or thereabouts. What was also peculiar is that, as the clearing got larger, many of the old and young members would come out and just stand in the sunlight. They stood with their faces pointed skywards at the sun; eyes closed and literally standing for hours soaking up the sun.

I can understand the feeling of the heat and comfort that the sun gives shining down on my own face, so I often stood among them. I enjoyed this time with members around me as we really didn't have much interaction during the winter months. Blue Eyes would always stand close to me with her elbow or shoulder touching me. She was fully grown now, but didn't quite look like the rest. Although she was sinewy and strong throughout her entire body, she didn't thicken up like the others and was eye to eye with me in height. I have always slept in my cabin while they secluded themselves through the winter so this was truly a gift for me.

I noticed that every single member of the tribe came out about mid-day to stand in the grass opening in the middle of the deep snow covered mountain side; every single day as if they had their clocks set to it. Once out in the opening they would all stand still with their faces towards the sun and make no sounds, no movement or interaction with one another. Looking around one afternoon I felt that I was standing among the world's most magnificent statues as they all stood motionless. Everyone would stand still, facing exactly the same way; it began to seem strange as a few days turned into a week of the same motionless behavior ensued. Two days in a row the clouds covered and the sun couldn't be seen but they still came out quietly and stood for about two hours; all facing the same direction and absolutely motionless. I couldn't imagine what had brought

on this behavior and why they were so pre-
cise about their timing but it sure brought
me reprieve in my winter months.

As if on cue they would all bring their
gaze back to their surroundings and file
silently back into the opening of the cave;
leaving me alone in the opening. It was odd
for a two hour visit in the open air but I was
appreciative for the activity during this cold
season. On the eleventh day; the sun was
bright and the clouds were nowhere to be
found and the crisp air was warming up in
the clearing. I waited quietly on the trail as
the members all filed out one by one to stand
in the open. I slowly wandered over and took
a position on the outside of the group, just
be among them again. I was not really interested in standing still in the cold for two
hours, but I thought the companionship
was worth the small discomfort of the cold.
Little Blue followed behind and made sure
we were standing close; this was comforting
and just what I needed. I was impressed by
their dedication and patience, holding still
for two hours in the cold. I spent most of

my time just watching them stand motionless as their breath made little puffs in the sunlight. I was almost to the point of losing interest when the group started getting restless as if something was about to happen. One of the females started to make an odd noise that triggered the rest of them. They all began to make soft sounds that can only be described as humming or exhaling with low tones like 'ahh' for lack of a better term. I was so engrossed in their noise that it didn't dawn on me that it had been getting darker by the minute.

Looking up I saw there wasn't a cloud in sight, but the light was fading fast and darkness was coming quick. Within fifteen minutes the sun had completely vanished and it was as dark as midnight. I was in the middle of an eclipse; the darkness in the middle of the day, surrounded by the low tones of the tribe made for a most remarkable event. As the light slowly came back the sounds of the tribe subsided and all became quiet as the moon passed completely out of the way. Again; as they had over the last ten days, the tribe all turned and slowly walked back into the darkness of their cave. They were gone, leaving me speechless and alone in the middle of the grass clearing. This had me thrilled, puzzled and in awe of what had just happened. The next day; not one single member emerged from the cave.

How on earth did they sense the coming of an eclipse, and how could they have known so early in advance to clear the grass for all members to witness it? These questions would never be answered for me; but I understood that it was time to start trusting the tribe's instincts when it came to the ways of nature. With no one coming outside, I made my way back to the cabin to write in my journal as these events were definitely worth remembering. The tribe had sensed a change in the environment and were able to forecast its occurrence; I was impressed with how could they have known a solar eclipse was on its way, so many days ahead.

I didn't see another tribe member throughout the rest of the winter; in fact they did not start emerging until the snow in the clearing had mostly melted. It was a late arrival for the tribe but the dynamic had changed up a little bit as well. Little Blue was every bit as tall as I was, and her face had become like that of an angel. The only way to describe her, is that she looked more like an adult human female with less body hair than anyone else in the tribe. Her face was bright and the cheek bones accented her strong jawline. By any standard on the planet, she was simply beautiful. She had the physique of an athlete who spent a lot of time building definition. The first time I saw her, Blue Eyes was briskly walking towards the cabin with two large portions of elk antlers in her hands; she was coming to hunt. As if we had never spent any time apart, we settled into the same routine with our hunting techniques. There was no Mrs. Frowny to chaperone; it was time to start earning our keep in the tribe. We would run on the trails leaving our area heading uphill for about three miles. Anything we caught up with and killed would be brought downhill for the greater portion of the trip.

This summer was different; she was a very fast runner and could out distance me with very little effort. Her stride was fluid and burst with power as she sprung forward. She was like watching a sprinter who didn't stop after a few hundred yards; she was tireless and kept looking over her shoulder waiting for me to catch up. I don't think she understood that she grew so quick and that I had remained the same; I would have to keep in shape and work on my stamina for the hunting ahead. I always tried to keep in shape and keep as active as I could; living out here on such a clean diet. If I wanted to continue to hunt with Little Blue, my conditioning and regiment was going to need an overhaul.

In the past we had counted on her nose and ears to locate any wildlife in the area long before we ducked into the trees. It was mostly rabbits and grouse that we caught, but today she had her sights on a small herd of deer in a small grove of aspen.

They were bedded down in the shade and had no idea we were within fifty yards behind them. We had never gone for big game before, it had always been the smaller animals. She crouched low and started to move, and from her actions the plan was the same as always. She would circle to the opposite side and literally run them towards me in hopes they would follow their normal, heavily used path. This was a pretty successful plan with rabbits and sage hens but I had my doubts on the deer. I would simply wait for the unsuspecting rabbit or bird to scramble by and literally bludgeon it with a piece of wood the size of a walking stick. Today the stakes were higher as she had thrust an antler in my hand and began to stalk her prey. I was dumbfounded as I stood on the side of an obvious game trail with a large length of antler in my hands. I had an idea that I was not anywhere close to being prepared for what lay ahead. It took only moments for Little Blue to get into position and start her approach towards the deer. She was within twenty yards of the herd when the entire group sprang up and split off in every different direction except for the trail; leaving my position beside the trail; useless.

Seeing the attempt had failed she turned to the closest one and gave chase instinctively. It only took a few seconds to realize that even with her strong stride, she was no match for the quickness of any one of the herd. I saw a hint of frustration in her face as she turned back towards me. I had no way of telling her that it was ok, as she hung her head like a scolded child. This was our first day out since last summer; it was time to go back to basics and start looking for rabbits as their fur was still white against the forest backdrop. By the end of the day we had pulled in a modest count of six rabbits before returning to the rock-slide area; a good days hunt for any tribe member. There were occasions when we would run into wolves in a pack; they were the only creatures that showed aggression toward the tribe members. Wolves in a pack were the most dangerous threat to the tribe's existence, and that was the only time I saw any members show fear or intimidation. I found it kind of strange that even a single lone wolf would attempt an attack on the much more dominate species, the canine would end up getting killed or injured and sent running to the trees. In our travels we saw two packs of wolves, one with twelve and the second only had seven. In each instance they were at a distance and we stayed out of their way.

The summer continued with hunting and fishing as Little Blue and I prepared for the winter months ahead. We never had another chance to bag a deer, but I felt confident that she hadn't forgotten, or would give up for that matter. The snow closed in quickly and my own winter hibernation began. I couldn't be penned up too long as the walls of the cabin offered little room for exercise and scenery. I spent several hours a day laboring through the deep snow with my snowshoes, trapping an occasional rabbit and even tried my hand at winter fishing. I had to stay occupied during the snow season to fight off the loneliness and cabin fever.

1980- Ashes to Ashes

The winter was short this year and the snow seemed to fade away quicker than usual which made for an earlier start into summer. I was able to spend more time with the tribe than I had anticipated; which worked out just fine for me. Little Blue and I settled into our rhythm of hunting for rabbits but I could tell that when she saw the big game, the temptation for bringing down one of the larger animals was definitely on her agenda.

We spent the first month doing a lot of chasing after the rabbits' and sage hens and brought in more than any other member. She had amazing speed and quick cat like movements when it came to pursuit. I, on the other hand, never mastered the art of leaping over four foot high logs and literally running down a rabbit with its sudden change of direction. We had a lot of eye contact when we would flank the prey which was our silent communication for the hunt.

One afternoon while she was circling around the far side of a small grove of trees; she spooked a young male deer that leapt to its feet and ran towards an opening to escape. This was the choice that would cost him his freedom as she had a much clearer path to the point of which he was headed. Her speed was explosive and her eyes narrowed with determination. Her ability to run in the trees had reached expert level, and could easily navigate around the few small trees that were in her way. The opening the deer was aiming for was crowded with the blue eyed warrior at the same time. With the left hand outstretched to grasp at its nose area she swung hard with her right that held the antler directing the blow to the side of its skull. Had the deer chosen a path running directly away from Little Blue he might have had a chance, but giving her an opportunity to intercept was the miscalculation that would cost him. That one fatal blow sealed the fate of the deer and brought them both crashing to the ground with a heavy thud. Like a flash she mounted the shoulders of the fallen deer and raised the antler for one more confirming blow. The time it took from the initial jump from its bed to the spot where the young buck now laid, was maybe ten seconds. This would be her first of many big game kills for the tribe.

Looking up for me was priceless, the look on her face was that of pride and accomplishment. I felt that a big hug and pat on the back might also get me an antler to the head; so I maintained my composure and smiled as best as I could with my eyes. We began packing her first big prize to the rockslide area.

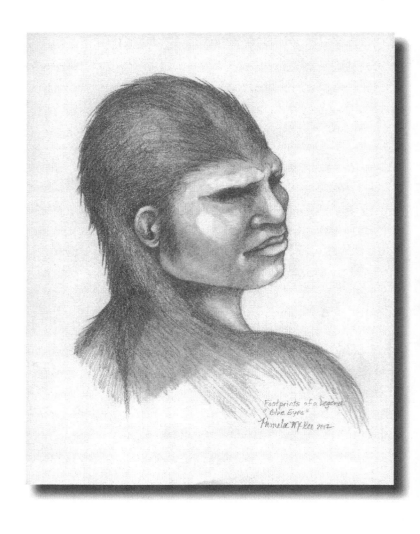

This fueled the fire for Little Blue as she had tasted the victory of a large kill; something she would become much more proficient with, even more than of any other tribal member. Little Blue didn't look like the other tribe members; her height had stopped at the six foot level. Her overall appearance was proportionate to her body as a well-muscled Olympic trainer. Her legs and calves were rigid and hard for exceptional speed and agility at a dead run; she could turn a corner at a full run and lose very little speed. The movements of Little Blue at a walk seemed lazy and almost tired; but in a flash she could spring into a full run that showed no signs of tiring out. She spent a good amount of time running and leaping through the heavy dense forest. It was as if she was a bird of prey soring effortlessly in the wind; only that same effortlessness was at a full speed run. It was a beautiful thing to watch as she recognized this as her strongest talent; she exercised it every time we left the area to hunt. Periodically she would take off at a sprint and simply not stop; I would sometimes wait for an hour or two after she had run out of sight. I would eventually give up and return to the cabin, there was no way of keeping up with her. It was just how she was; wild and absolutely free. It was better to let her run; waiting for a slow poke like me would certainly slow her down. She would come back to the cabin from the rock-slide area the next morning looking ready for a new adventure. As usual I began the morning with the traditional greetings; "Good morning, Little Blue" and then pointed to myself and said, "John Stone." This morning we were preparing to leave the cabin when the male, with the scar on his face came over from the rock-slide as if to join the two of us on our hunt. Little Blue looked warily and hissed at him with obvious disapproval but he continued to linger behind as we started up the trail. She even rushed at him and swept up a handful of dirt and threw it towards him as if to scare him away. He simply fell in behind us as if he was part of the overall plan but Little Blue was not going to have any part of that. Like a flash she circled around me and with clenched fists at her shoulders she ran into his chest with both of her elbows; knocking the wind from his lungs. If that was not enough, he had lost his balance when his heel caught the side of the trail and he landed squarely on his butt. Instinctively, he lunged forward with outstretched hands and hit Little Blue in the chest; knocking her backwards into the grass. Before anyone could react, Little Blue had scrambled to her feet and lunged once again towards the larger male and thrust the top of her head into the mouth of the male with a loud smack. This snapped his head backwards and blood flowed immediately from his split lip. Now in pain, and bleeding, the male lunged towards the female again; only to come up empty handed. The fast moving female had eluded the attack and now stood about five feet away as if to taunt the larger male. Her eyes were bright and alive with anger, but it was easy to see she was already calculating her next move. His position was not about to be challenged; with a loud breath he gave chase towards the much quicker female who easily out maneuvered him. With his temper rising, he lunged again to run after her; as fast as he was, there was no way he would ever catch Little Blue. I don't know if this bad blood between the two stems from something that happened within the cave, possibly a court-ship of sorts. I also wondered if Little Blue was being protective of her time with me. My hunt would be put on hold for the day as I watched the female disappear over the crest of the hill with an unhappy bleeding male in hot pursuit.

The chase must have gotten Little Blue's point across as the male with the scar never showed up for another early morning prepa-ration at the cabin. We continued to hunt together for food, and her talent for bringing deer down became her specialty, which in these mountains were plentiful. One morn-ing we left the cabin at sunrise and stopped on the top of the ridge-line for a few min-utes to watch the beautiful colors caress out across the darkness and bring a new day of exploring and hunting on the back side of the mountain from the rock-slide. We would run a ten mile loop on our round about travels. A big game kill at this distance would mean plenty of work, but we were up for the challenge. Watching Little Blue take in the fresh air and cover the distance with her fluid movements was like getting caught up in the enjoyment of someone who discovers new surprises and radiates that happiness. We had been on the trail for a couple of hours when Little Blue stopped in her tracks with her eyes towards the far away hill side. Her hands were out in front of her as if reaching into the darkness and her eyes were not focusing in at anything on that hill side. With a loud sigh she dropped to the ground on her hands and knees as if feeling her way on the ground.

This behavior caught me off guard as I had never seen this kind of thing before. I had no idea what was happening to Little Blue; it looked like she was in pain and maybe suffering from some kind of health issue. I immediately stepped in and dropped to a knee at her side placing my hand on her forearm and the other on her back. She tensed up like a spring and brought her eyes up to look into my face. It occurred to me that this was the first time I had physically touched Little Blue since the first year when she was a child. Realizing this might be a huge mistake I snapped my hands back from her and sat back to allow some distance between us. Her eyes said it all; she was physically alright but there was something wrong. She crawled forward and grabbed my wrist and placed my hand on the ground as if to make me feel the soil. Her face was upset and her posture showed that she was anxious to leave this place right away. Standing up quickly she started down the trail back towards the rock-slide; two hours from here. Her pace was very difficult to keep up with; I found myself running, trying to keep up most of the time, but the elevation and steep inclines prevented me from keeping pace. She would slow down and wait from time to time; not willing to leave me behind as she had done in the past. Something was different with this trip back to the rock-slide. She literally passed up an easy target rabbit and pressed on; this was a task that would have taken less than two minutes.

I was relieved to finally reach the glacier above the cabin knowing that we were within a couple hundred yards of home. She broke off towards the rock-slide for about ten yards and stopped; almost irritated that I did not follow her in that direction. Confused by her actions I hesitated, but decided that I did not want to second guess her intent so I complied and turned to follow her to the rocks. Getting over the rocks and to the entrance of the cave was fluid and easy for her as she leapt from rock to rock; for me it was a bit more challenging. Several tribe members were out in the grassy clearing pulling up grass by the handfuls and stacking up piles of grass and greenery. Most of the items being picked were not edible; other members would come in and grab arm loads of the vegetation and rush towards the cave entrance carrying their grass. This was not food supply for winter months in mid spring; it was a preparation for something for inside the cave, possibly for comfort. Were they expecting others from afar to come to this place and preparing bedding?

Looking off in the horizon it appeared that a storm was coming in from the west; weathering a storm from the depths of a solid stone cave should be no problem for this tribe. Nothing was adding up yet, but I believe that it would reveal itself soon enough. I had seen enough of this production and turned to head back to the cabin. Little Blue barked from down in the clearing which caught my attention. I could tell she was communicating with me as she was looking directly at me. The sound was awkward but definitely sounded like 'Stone.' I did not yet understand; but felt this had to be serious and I had better wait this one out. She turned and looked uphill and barked out a series of two commands and looked back at me. What I did see was the male with the scar coming down the slope towards my position with me in his sights. As he approached, the male reached out for my elbow and turned me towards the cave entrance and fell in behind me; obviously he wanted me to go into the cave again. The thought of going inside that cave was revolting; looking back, there was nothing inviting about it. Whatever storm was coming could be weathered out in my cabin so I stopped and waited. The clouds were coming in closer but there was no wind to speak of; it was odd as the clouds approaching were solid on the horizon like a big wall. Another loud bark from the clearing and a rough nudge from behind was all I needed to know that I really had no choice in the matter.

I stood at the entrance of the cave taking in the foul odors coming from within. The thought of ducking my head and stepping into the darkness with these tribe members had me fighting claustrophobia in the worst way. I was not all that fond of confinement and today I was just expected to embrace it with the company of giants. Little Blue was just coming up behind me, this gave slight comfort about going in; but I didn't have to be happy about it. The rest of the members were closing in from the grassy clearing with the last of the grass in their arms. It appeared that all members were coming indoors to get away from this storm, the clouds were dark like that of an incoming tornado. As I came in, the room had a few stragglers but the area inside was mostly clear with the exception of the older large male, the male with the scar, Little Blue, myself and another young male. Once the young male came in with his arm load of grass and vegetation the three males started placing rocks in the entrance of the cave and putting grass between the stones to block both the wind and sound. The entrance was sealed up with an air tight door within minutes; leaving me literally standing in the dark. The light from the opening on the left had been blocked off as well. Off to my left the gentle hands of Little Blue wrapped around my arm and pulled me to the side wall where I could feel her sitting towards the floor pulling me down with her. She leaned heavily on me with a big sigh; this was the most physical contact I have had in years. It was cold, dark, scary and yet wonderful; Little Blue was my closest companion and I couldn't be more content with her trust.

I spent the next three days and nights in the blackness of the cave; locked within the walls of the hard, cold, dark, musty, stinky prison cell of a space. Not only was this the second visit to the cave; it was not my idea of a fun sleep over. The only comfort was the presence of Little Blue; who always stayed within contact. Food was brought to us; but we had to walk the narrow passage of the cave to the right that led to the running water. The stone ceiling was low at one point, and I had a small warning as Little Blue who was leading me through the pitch black pulled me lower. She held my hand and placed my other hand on her hip so that I could feel her direction in the darkness. She would lean forward and crouch low to avoid the low solid ceiling. I only had to hit my forehead once to learn; when she leaned down, I leaned down. We made it to the water for drinking every five or six hours and I must say that the water was cold, pure and amazing. The food that was brought was cold and raw but the lingering smell of elk meat told me what I was eating when I chewed on its chilly rubbery substance. I had gotten used to the diet of green leaves and raw fish and game and felt healthier than ever. I did get my tour of the path to the left; we traveled back along its flat surface for maybe 50 yards before stopping. I was aware of a stench that became stronger and more powerful the further we went. This had me almost gagging by the time she stopped moving. I had no idea how big the room was that we were in; the echoes told me that it was a very large space. There was a small trickle of water close to my feet, but she stopped me in my tracks. The next thing she did was move a couple of steps away and stop; I could hear her urinating on the hard floor and understood right away. This was the bathroom of the cave... This cleared up a lot of things for me as I took this opportunity to relieve my own bladder. I smiled to myself as I thought of how the air quality or lack thereof in this room made my eyes burn. It was pitch black; why did I even have my eyes open? This schedule went on for two days; the third day I was taken towards the sound of the water. With Little Blue holding my hand, we traveled down the path to the right towards the water; drank our fill and continued beyond. The running water, which traveled in from the right to the left flowing at a pretty good pace. The flow was maybe four feet across and tapered in from both sides to a middle depth reaching almost to my knee caps.

This was a significant distance to travel with the path veering off to the right. I was able to see gray colors ahead which led to an opening in the distance. There was a slight incline for the last fifty yards; up to a straight shotgun barrel of a path. I could finally see light in the distance and smiled to myself thinking "This was literally: the light at the end of the tunnel." As we came within twenty feet from the opening, the room opened wide on both sides and led straight out to the rear exit of the cave. The opening to the outside was roughly fifteen feet wide; at the highest point, five to six feet in the middle and closing out both sides.

There was some brush and vines around the opening; it was inviting to finally see an exit. Covering the floor was a gray dust that got deeper the closer we approached to the opening. Within five feet from the opening Little Blue stopped me from continuing any further. I knelt down and touched the powdery like substance and found it to stick together like powdered sugar or flour, it certainly wasn't snow. I looked out the opening, there appeared to be a heavy fog in the air as sight was limited to just a few yards. I had no way of knowing what was beyond that opening; I couldn't see anything. The air inside the opening was hazy too, and I realized that it was not fog at all, but a fine dust or ash that was settling. This was ash from a fire somewhere in the forest; it had to be. How could they have known about a forest fire so far out? I shuddered to think of a fire taking out all the trees and me being trapped in the cabin as it destroyed everything in its path. The ash was over an inch deep on the ledge of the opening; my life had been spared by Little Blue. I coughed a few times and noticed that the more we moved around that we were stirring up more of the fine ash; it was time to retreat back into the cave to a cold dark space and wait for the ash to settle, something I didn't think I would ever choose to do. Before leaving I noticed several other openings that went back into the mountain but our fresh tracks in the ash told me what direction we were headed back to. Holding the hand of my blue eyed warrior I followed her into the depths of darkness towards the sound of running water.

The next few days and nights all ran together with a whirlwind of unanswered questions; I knew it had to be May of 1980 according to my month and year tracking. If our forest was gone, the wildlife and vegetation would not be enough to sustain the demands of this tribe. Unless there was another home for this family; an event like this could lead to their extinction. They need a location that provided room to hide this many family members. A home positioned in an area rich enough with vegetation and wildlife for food, also the demand for remaining invisible as this was the key to their existence.

Finally there was noise by the front entrance where I had been sleeping on the hard floor with Little Blue. The first tiny ray of light came through as the first stone was pulled away. A flurry of ash danced into the room as the light took away the blackness that had been our existence for the last several days. The next stone removed made a much larger opening that filled the room with light, leaving us all blinking and rubbing our sensitive eyes. I was never more excited to see daylight and to be free from the confines of the solid stone open room. Stepping out into the light was slow going at first as the brightness made it difficult to keep our eyes open. Not only was the sun shining through but the ground was covered with a light gray ash that reflected the brightness; much like snow covered ground.

The trees were not burned, the forest still stood in front of me; our mountain had been spared. The entire range in front of me had remained untouched from any fire. There must have been a fire somewhere close enough to have left so much ash on the ground. It was everywhere as far as the eye could see. Walking in the gray covering created billowing clouds of ash with each and every step. There was no escaping the mess; it was on every surface. Everything looked as if it was covered with gray snow, the ground, trees, rocks and my home. The next few weeks were spent cleaning out my cabin as even with the closed doors; the fine ash had reached through to the inside of my sturdy home and left everything covered in gray.

Within two months the ash was less obvious as the few rains and wind carried it away. It was still everywhere in the forest, but nature had a way of cleaning up its mess and allowing new growth to come through. The wildlife suffered more than most as the food supply was buried under a layer of ash that couldn't have been good for their lungs or the digestive system. Even the water took its own loss as the streams and rivers were the vehicle to take away the ash from the mountain after the rains. It also deprived the fish from clean water as the streams carried a silvery film that was heavy with ash. But even through it all; the earth was able to start healing itself and things did get back to normal. It was quiet back at the rockslide and in my cabin. The wildlife found their food, the tribe found their rhythm and Little Blue and I resumed our hunting; life was as it should be.

The Bully

There seemed to be a rhythm with the tribe that never stopped; there was hunting, gathering supplies and storing it deep within the cave. It appeared to be a normal family life with the adults mentoring their young in the ways of the wilderness. The winters and summers flew by so quickly that it all seemed to run together into one long camping trip. I have been around this tribe for going on fifteen years now, and seen plenty of interaction between the members. If you were to look at them as every day normal families; you might just expect to see them sending the children off to school, and the discipline was never more than a hiss or a deep guttural bark that quickly caught the attention of the younger generation. There was none of the 'testing' of the children with their parents. A growl or grunt meant that the next thing coming was going to sting, putting a stop to the nonsense quickly. As with every normal family there were the typical bickering and disputes that would grow quickly and get physical between the male members, more than with the females. One day I witnessed an episode escalate between two young males that became vicious and more brutal than anything I had ever witnessed. The larger of two young adult males was jet black in color, he was more perfectly sculpted than I had ever seen. He was almost six feet already and had proved himself as an exceptional hunter. He was kind of pushy and as far as culture goes, and had the least amount of manners. The smaller male was the son of the male with the red hair. This smaller member was also the one and only offspring of the red haired male. The red male had grown over the years into one of the strongest members of the tribe. As an adult he was the thickest and scariest one of the tribe; and he still treated me with distain.

The young male with the jet black hair was continuously badgering the smaller male, and never seemed to let up. The harassment continued to the point that the smaller male had his fill and finally turned and slapped him on the side of the face hitting the ear with a solid thump. The sound alone echoed through the area and drew immediate attention from the others. The larger male lunged at the smaller male who tried to move away quickly, but was standing too close to avoid the outstretched hands of the larger male. Once he knew he had a grip on his smaller opponent; the larger male pulled him in close and sank his teeth into the top of the shoulder by the neck and pulled away a thumb size piece of flesh. A shrill scream erupted from the smaller male's mouth and frantically he pushed into the chest of the large male trying to free himself from his tight grip.

Against the strength of the large male, the smaller ones efforts were futile as the larger male 'toyed' with his captive minimizing his efforts to struggle against his great power. This is the kind of incident that would be likened to a big brother antagonizing the younger brother, only with much more serious consequences. At this point the smaller male thrust his head forward towards the larger males face, thumping his hard skull into the black male's nose; breaking the cartilage at the base of the nose. The cracking sound and impact on his face snapped his head back slightly, stunning the male. His grip gave slightly, but his hands never let go of the smaller male as the pain and smell of his own blood enraged the larger male. Pushing the smaller opponent away from his chest still firmly gripping the helpless youth; the larger male drew him quickly, into his own forehead, and returned the head butt into the face of the smaller male. There was the sound of cracking caused by the nose cartilage and visibly breaking the brow line bone over the right eye of the younger male. With a gasp and exhale the smaller male was rendered unconscious and limp in the hands of the larger male. By now the adult females in the area were moving their way towards this dispute, the attention it was getting was not going to be positive.

Still in pain the black male decided that he had not inflicted enough pain on the smaller male so again he butted his head into the already swollen and bleeding youth with a loud crack; splitting the front of the younger males face even wider. With a loud bark, the younger male's mother came running in from two hundred yards away at full speed, trying to get to the area quickly. Seeing that big trouble was on the way the male dug his teeth in again into the neck of the younger male pulling away with vital life sustaining arteries, and dropped the lifeless male to the ground. Seeing that the larger female was almost upon them, the black male turned with amazing speed, running towards the rock-slide area. Within a hundred feet of the slide the red haired male came into view, and the fleeing black male redirected his course to a downhill path away from their home.

Not knowing what had just occurred, the red male watched in curiosity as the male continued to run from view and down into the valley below. A loud bark from the mother of their only offspring caught his attention and he continued in hast towards her side. He stopped just short of the scene where his only son laid lifeless on the ground. His eyes widened with disbelief as he took in the view of his female mate kneeling beside his baby boy; piecing together what had just taken place. Looking over at the tree line where the young male had fled, he let out an ear-splitting bark followed by a soul wrenching howl that echoed through the valley below. This was his warning; this fight would not be over until he had settled the score.

He stayed by his mate; he did not leave her to rush out and exact his revenge. His mate needed him now, tonight they would bury their only son; murdered at the hands

Footprints of a Legend "Red" Pamela McKee 2012

of a bully. There was a funeral procession that brought out all the tribe members minus one; a pure black youth whom had disappeared. The young bully had run; he was the one that had fled from the tribe after causing the unthinkable for the red colored father. I don't think this was the last of it; there would be a price to pay. During the funeral the members were affected like never before. The mourning of the tribe was longer and the trench stayed open for an hour as the tribe waited for the large red male and his mate to stand up after kneeling beside their son. As they made their way back to the upper flat rock, they both looked worn down and defeated. This family put their heart and soul into the life and unity they had here; essentially they lost two members that afternoon. Little Blue carried stones with the rest of the tribe; every member was present, doing their share. The older male that I had first met so many years ago was mostly silver, but did not look old. He was clearly still the Alpha and without a doubt the leader of the tribe. His hair showed his age but his body was still shaped like a power lifter. Over the years I had been witness to several funerals; I must say that this one had the most profound effect on the tribe.

There was a sadness that loomed over the tribe with the loss of the young male like I had never seen before. The few young that were around were quiet and the activity that flourished in the summer months had slowed down to an agonizing pace. Little Blue and I continued to hunt throughout the region and contributed plenty of winter supplies to the tribe as the winter closed in.

Company from Afar

Over the next five years, our routine was the same with summer time and winter months. As isolated as I was in the winter; knowing that summer was coming was the only real light at the end of the tunnel for me. I counted on Little Blue for companionship and guidance around the tribe as she was the interpreter for our communication. We were evolving as the time spent became more educational. There were summers that Little Blue would take off running while we were out and not return. I understood this as her way of keeping the free spirit inside her satisfied. She was physically very attractive with her brilliant eyes, high cheekbones and strong jawline full of bright white teeth. Often we would get a couple of miles away and sit on a ledge overlooking the open range and I would simply talk to her while pointing things out and saying what they were. It was on one of these excursions that Little Blue looked at me with her bright blue eyes and spoke out loud, "Joh-on". It was incredible as she turned my name into a two syllable word, and I was thrilled to hear it. So I repeated it back to her with a gesture towards myself, "John Stone".

"Joh-on Stone" was crystal clear as she gleamed with pride, seeing the excitement in my eyes.

Our dialog was interrupted with a howl in the distance towards the rock-slide that had

Little Blue scrambling to her feet and moving out towards her home at a pace that I could never keep up with. I simply followed at my best pace knowing that eventually I would catch up to the speedy warrior. We hadn't traveled too far from the cave so it shouldn't take long to get back to the rock-slide. In the distance I could hear the sound of members fighting in the brush that was filled with growls and snapping of branches. I was still a good mile away from the rock-slide but this area was still familiar. There were several members in the trees that I could see close to a small clearing occupied by three males. These were males that I had never seen before as they looked different from the rock-slide family. One was the young pure black male who had taken the life of the young son of the red male. He was now fully grown; much taller with stronger features and much denser throughout his body. The other two with him were large in size but not as big as the ones from this tribe; maybe from another area? The two males were filthy with red dirt and their hair was matted and unkempt. They were not native to the area as they put off their own distinct odor; much like that of a sanitary landfill and petroleum mixed with septic waste. The tribe here had their earth skunky smell as well; but this was overpowering or maybe I had just gotten used to the constant odor. One of the visitors was carrying a four foot metal piece of pipe from a water line with an elbow still attached. It was odd seeing the man-made materials out here in the hands of a Bigfoot. Just the sight of the metal pipe in their hands put the entire scene out of place. The other was carrying a length of antler as was the pure black male. They were not here for a social visit; but were here looking for trouble. The growling was coming from the black male as he displayed aggression towards everyone in the trees with his behavior. He was kicking at the brush and charging short distances towards the members of the tribe but stopping just shy of making contact. His behavior was interesting in the fact that he continued to slap at his chest and thighs in anger; trying to provoke the others. The impact of his slap clapped into the air like shots from a rifle. His taunting was violent and loud as he rushed back and forth. The two males that accompanied him were startled at the sight of me and withdrew quickly into the brush as if to hide. This left the male in the clearing alone and without backup. Without his friends to back him; the aggression took a different tone as the members of the rock-slide stepped into the clearing. There were four members; one of which was Little Blue. The large red male was nowhere to be found; I am guessing that he was hunting far away or deep within the cave and had no idea that his opportunity to settle the score was so close to home.

The two filthy males had simply vanished; leaving the male outnumbered and vulnerable. Not one of the tribe members charged or made any gesture to attack; except Little Blue. She ran in quickly and did not stop; she sped by and hit the male on the side of the temple with her antler and continued to the other side of the clearing where she stopped to look back. Stunned by the blow the male dropped to one knee with a groan; leaving another opportunity for Little Blue. She came back wielding the antler high, hitting him directly in the nose splitting the skin wide open on the bridge with a loud smack. The male simply fell backwards in a heap.

Little Blue was now standing on the other side of the clearing. No one had touched the pure black male except for Little Blue. He was a mess and yet he regained his footing and was standing in the clearing, blood flowing from his face. The scene in front of me was fascinating as the male had been hit twice by Little Blue and he was powerless to do a thing about it. Little Blue made her way around the circle to stand next to me. The male in the clearing stood still; glaring with hatred at the others. We all stood silent for a good twenty seconds before everyone just backed into the trees; including Little Blue and myself. Her speed was efficient and lightning fast, she had perfected her skills with the horn.

We left the wounded male standing alone in the clearing. He did not have a home on this mountain range; that point had been made perfectly clear.

Nights in the Den

Two years passed with the continued basic hunting in the summers with Little Blue and me gathering supplies for the winters. I had developed a taste for raw fish and elk but the gamy taste of deer still hadn't been acquired. We saw almost every sunrise and sunset together over the years when she was not in her cave during the winter months. Our dialog was building with several words but I found her resistant to use her voice in my language. I kept forgetting that she was not a human by genetics with her features and constant companionship making the line pretty blurred. She would say few words in her voice; and when she did, it always amazed me. Her voice was low and soft as she strained to control the sound of the word. Her eyes were constantly alert to whatever I was doing or studying how I did things. She was an incredible student towards my ways; I believe I had learned much more from her over the years.

She spent a lot of time touching the cloth of my shirt and would often come in close to smell my skin and garments. She was very comfortable with sitting close and being in contact with me as she leaned heavily on me. I always knew that when I sat down, I had better be in a good solid position as she would lean in and use me for her very own personal back rest. The time was filled with days of hunting and endless hours together of exploring the vast mountain ranges that lay at our disposal.

One week we had wandered off our normal area and worked our way through a large dense basin full of signs of deer and elk. This could be a great place to hunt later on in the year when the temperatures got cooler. I stopped for a second as the surroundings seemed familiar but I couldn't quite place why. It was five minutes later when I discovered a moccasin print in the soft earth that immediately put chills up and down my spine; revealing why I had known this place. We needed to get out of here; I was within a half mile of the camp site of the two mountain men that I wanted nothing to do with. They were not the kind of folks that would understand the blue eyed female at my side. I reached out and put my finger on my lips in the 'shh' shape and she nodded in acknowledgment as we turned around and headed off the trail. I wanted distance more than anything so I headed south east away from our rock-slide location for about five miles; it was getting dark and we would be staying the night soon as we had done in the past. We then changed our direction north for the next three miles before darkness prevented us from going any further, there were too many clouds for us to move successfully in moonlight. We spent the night huddled up beside some cliffs where the only access was to approach from over a small stream of slow moving water. Anything coming close would make plenty of noise in the water and give us advanced warning. About halfway through the night I could have sworn that I heard voices off in the distance. I know Little Blue heard it too as she sat upright and turned her ear toward the sound; but it did not continue. This was a mistake I did not care to repeat; I had to avoid this area as nothing good could ever come from it.

The next day we returned back to the cabin where instead of going to the cave Little Blue just leaned against the wall of the cabin in the sun and showed no indication of leaving. I took the opportunity to test her good nature and sat down beside her and leaned heavily on her shoulder. She didn't budge; in fact I woke up after quite a long nap to still be resting on her. I smiled as I sat up feeling honored that she would rather spend her time with me today, over going to her home.

When nightfall came, Little Blue came over to me and helped me to my feet and pulled at my arm signaling me to follow her to the cave. Thinking nothing of the gesture, I filed in behind her on the trail managing my way over the rocks towards the entrance with Little Blue. At the entrance she ducked in a few feet and waited for me to follow her into their foul smelling home. Once inside Little Blue took my hand and led me to the path on the right and we headed towards the sound of water. Reaching the running water I held on to her hand tightly and stayed close as we took two steps into the running water to the other side. In the pitch dark I could only imagine how much water passed through there in a day. The water moved pretty quick; fast enough to churn loudly in the cave. We continued on towards the end of the cave to the other side. It took about forty five minutes before I could see any signs of light; at least this time I knew the destination and the trip was not new.

Once in the open room by the exit of the cave I was able to see much better as the light from the outside was shining in. This experience was clearer and the air was not obstructed with all the ash from early in 1980. This was my second time in this portion of the cave and I was curious to see what was beyond the opening. To my surprise Little Blue put her hand out and stopped me from walking over to the exit so I could look out.

"Joh-on Stone" she said quietly and pulled me to the ground into a crawling position. On our hands and knees she crawled in front of me and led me to the opening. As I got closer I realized why she didn't want me to walk over to the opening. We were high up on a sheer rock wall. There was nothing beyond that wall but open space and a serious drop of five or six hundred feet straight down. I laid flat on my stomach taking in the fresh air and the breathtaking scenery that lay in front of me. This would not be a viable exit by any means unless you came here with a parachute. The sheer face wall offered protection from predators on this side of the mountain. We must have laid there for a half hour just taking it all in; it was magnificent.

She took my arm and stood me up to lead me back towards one of the openings that led into another room. This room was covered in grass circles that looked like oversized nests or beds for animals to sleep in; or tribe members. She stepped into a small circle of dried grass and vegetation and gestured for me to settle into one adjacent to it. Accepting the invitation I gingerly stepped in and sat down on the thick padding. It felt nice actually, and after leaning over I could see why they would sleep in the nests; they were quite comfortable. The light was fading fast in the room and Little Blue reached her arm over and held my arm with both her hands. Apparently I was sleeping in the cave tonight; something I never would have expected. One by one the others came in and settled into their perspective beds and moved around until they had found their comfortable position. Not one of them showed any surprise that I was in the room; a pretty good feeling. This room housed seven members and the sounds in the night were filled with the snoring of giants. It was amazing how much noise these members made in the solid sound proof room; this was a first for me. Morning light came and slowly they all made their way out of the room; including Little Blue and I. The open air was a welcome luxury after spending the night in the cave with the others but I had a suspicion that it wouldn't be my last. There was a good feeling waking up in the cave with all the strange sounds and unsavory smells, with the acceptance having finally reached a new level.

Little Blue brought me there often to sleep and keep her company a couple days each week. If I wasn't brought there by her; I stayed put in the cabin in the comfort of my own home. The comfort of having me around the tribe got to the point that I didn't even raise an eye from anyone when I was near; I felt like I had actually become one of their family members. Even the two large males, one with the red hair and the other with a scar appeared to tolerate my company. They even were responsible for bringing a nice size deer to my cabin and leaving it outside for my winter supplies. I enjoyed the surroundings of my own cabin, but also relished in the company of Little Blue as she always insisted on holding on to my arm or hand; it was the touch that we both needed.

Black Water

One late afternoon Little Blue came to get me from the cabin and the two of us headed to the cave entrance for the evening. We walked a few steps down the right path and Little Blue stopped. She put her hand on my back and gently pushed me on as she turned around and headed back towards the entrance. This was an indication for me to continue on without her and she would meet me in the sleeping chamber at the other side of the cave. It was strange making my way without my guide as I literally had to slide my hands on the hard walls to find my way towards the water and then beyond. I didn't want to feel my way into one of the tribal members who might be in a rush to get out as I would certainly be trampled without any effort on their part. Hearing the water was a good indication for the first part as I continued toward the sound of the rushing stream. Finally it was right under my feet as I could feel the tiny droplets of water soak into my shoes. My first step went into the freezing water covering just over my ankles. I reached out in front as I knew the ceiling was low at this point and found it to be less than an inch from my face; it was a close call from smacking my face in the rock. It was pitch black in here and this was much more difficult without my tour guide, but I was doing alright so far. The water was moving fast so I took my next step into the darkness and placed my foot deeper into the rushing water. Putting my weight forward and leaning under the low ceiling, my hand on the surface slipped and I pitched forward into the running water. I put both hands out and landed in the crawling position with my face in the water, and unable to gather my balance. There was nothing to reach for stability and I felt the water pulling me to the left as I fought the current. I did not have enough of my body above the water to have any foundation even while on my knees so the water pulled me head first into the darkness dragging me under the surface.

I sucked in a deep breath as I felt the pressure of the water pushing me deeper into the dark stream. I couldn't fight the speed in which the water was carrying me into the cave but I knew I was well beyond the path that I was once on. I was being carried into a tunnel underground that was narrow at some points and had steep smooth walls that provided nothing to grab hold of. I was moving fast with the current and could not stop my decent. It was much like a slide on a playground with water pushing you through. Most of the bottom and sides were deep and solid as I tried to turn my body around. The idea of swimming head first in an underground stream could not end well. Finally there was a wide spot that I was able to grab hold of a small outcropping just long enough that my feet finally swung around in front, unable to hold on, my wet hands slipped away. I was now moving feet first into the darkness with no idea where I would end up. I was panicking as I did not want to drown in this dark, wet, underground tunnel. My hands were getting cut up with the speed in which I was traveling and I had hit my head on the low surface several times, almost knocking me out. There was always the labored task of catching a breath; not knowing when I would be trying to inhale, my head would be forced underwater as my speed was increasing with the flow of the stream. I put one hand down in front of me trying to protect myself and the other arm over my head with my elbow up to shield my face from hitting the rocks. I inhaled enough water over the last few minutes and considered that I was living my last moments. The desire to survive was kicking in and the realization that I could very well lose my life in this tunnel was making me fight even harder than ever. I could hear loud water ahead and I couldn't do a thing to slow down my speed; it was a possibility that this was a waterfall that would smash me into the underground rocks below?

It turned out to be a very narrow passage where the water literally rushed through to the depths beyond. I had just taken a deep breath when the walls on either side of me narrowed and pinched me to a stop; several inches below the surface. I reached with my hand in front and realized that the ceiling was holding my arm down and I was too far in to use my upper hand to pull myself in either direction. I was trapped as my body was physically plugging the hole. Completely submerged, I struggled to hold onto my breath while my ears felt like they were going to pop from the pressure. I had no way to get another breath; the water was not stopping, this would be my last exhale. The pressure was increasing as the water behind me was rushing in. I still stubbornly held that breath; exhaling tiny portions at a time thinking it would make me last. I am stubborn, but this is one of those things you cannot prepare for, and instinctively I held on to that last bit of air. I had to give up; I needed to quit fighting and surrender to nature's way of putting me to rest. With my eyes bulging out and my blood desperate for oxygen I decided to allow most of my breath to escape vowing that I would not inhale as I was completely under water and submit to the elements. In a flash my body rushed forward and the next three seconds it shot-gunned me through ten or fifteen feet of sheer rock tunnel out into a wide space where I was able to suck in several gasps of air. I was still moving fast through the channel but for the first time I saw light from somewhere ahead. It sped past over head with an opening that was above my head six or seven feet. From my quick look at it; the opening seemed like it was not big enough to put a lunch pail through. Just as quickly, it disappeared behind me.

Suddenly I burst out into the open light, tumbling sideways across the rocks at the base of a small waterfall. The little underground stream had just spit me out at the base of a rock formation into a large mountain stream. Blinded by the sudden light I scrambled to grab something solid enough to stop my moving and clung to a large rock at the edge of the churning water. Still gasping for the clean air I pulled myself out onto the gravel and sand away from the current and rolled over on my back. I was terrified, cut, bruised, bleeding, exhausted, and soaking wet but smiling. I was thankful to be alive and had no idea where I had ended up, but was thrilled to know that I could get out of the cave through the running water if ever trapped. It would be my last choice for sure but it was good to know.

After a half hour of just lying in the setting sun and drying off I sat up to find a place to camp for the night. I was simply worn down from the trauma and close call; I needed to rest. I nestled up next to a big pine tree with some thick shrubs behind me; I am sure I would have rested better in the cabin, but this would have to do for tonight. The next morning I headed north east up the side of a dense mountain covered with blueberry bushes and literally ate my way up the side of the mountain. Once on top I got my bearings and circled around into familiar territory and back towards my cabin. I was going to enjoy some fresh meat and catch up on some much needed sleep in the comfort of my own bed. Little Blue was there in the grass, waiting in the warm summer sun; I walked past my cabin front door and sat down next to her, leaning heavily on her shoulder.

The next three days I stayed close to the cabin gathering vegetation to store in the glacier for the winter months. Little Blue never left my side and slept against the outside wall of the cabin each night, giving up her own comforts to be near me. I gave her a couple of hides and left my cabin door and shutters open while she was there. My blueberry supplies were filling up nicely, this season yielded plenty of vegetation for winter inventory. For a reminder of the lessons learned in the stream within the cave, I carved a little note for myself in the cross beam of the cabin. Stepping back I admired my note in the wood; 'The only way out is in'.

Big Ears

I had been watching one of the young females over the last several years from maybe 1999 to now; in 2001 and the interaction between her and the scarred male. They often would sit close and lean on each other; but as far as how I have seen other couples interact, they were not as obvious. They reminded me of high school sweethearts trying to keep their relationship secret from others. This went on for two summers and I finally saw the results of their courtship as the female was pregnant with a baby when they stepped out for their summer months after a long winter. She was far enough along that I estimated that we would see the youngster before the next winter closed in.

It was back to business as usual for me, the hunting continued with Little Blue for the next couple of months where she would often race after a herd of deer or elk and not return for two days. She was never gone for more than one night and like an uneasy parent on prom night I would watch the horizon waiting for her return. When she would run; I would head back home if she didn't come back within a couple of hours or if night was approaching fast. More often than not, she would come back with bloodied hands and the look of a proud beautiful warrior. It was difficult to look at her as a tribe member; she looked to me like a beautiful woman. She had short hair all over her entire body like the others; only much less of it. Her face had less hair than the others; not thick and covering but fine and almost nonexistent. I was her closest companion, as not one single male in the tribe paid her any real attention.

I didn't know if I had taken the role of her partner, or if I was preventing her from finding her tribal mate. I didn't want to give up my time with her; but I also couldn't bear the thought of robbing her of true love. In fact, I did love her, but I was uncertain where relationships like ours could ever evolve to, we were just so perfectly suited for each other, that it could get confusing. We didn't need more than what we had as far as I could see; time would tell if she needed more, and I would need to be willing to step away so she could find her mate within her tribe.

I was not at all surprised when Little Blue came to the cabin early one morning to take me back to the cave to see the little addition to the tribe. The adult male with the scar and his female companion were leaning in over a young male that had just been introduced into the tribe. At birth they had hair all over; black thick hair that covered their entire body, like a sheep dog almost. This little one had big fat cheeks and tiny little hands that circled around the fingers of the proud and exhausted female. It was the same as looking at human parents with a newborn baby. The male looking up at all the members present, for that acknowledgement and confirmation. The mother looked worn out from the birth and was settling in for the nursing portion of the child's new life. This little male was big for a baby; close to two feet long. His face was hairy, but what stood out the most, were his ears... I had never seen a bigger set of ears on anything in my life. I couldn't help it; but I was calling this one 'Big Ears'. Even the father with the scar allowed me close to the infant, letting me touch its little feet and face. I loved the opportunity to see the newest addition to the tribe.

I enjoyed Big Ears as he was a ball of curiosity and shadowed my every move. I was around from the early stages of his life so the oddness of me not being one of the tribe was never really an issue for him. His comfort level with me as a family member was never questioned. I found that he would lean on me as only one other tribal member did. It was something that also made a bridge for closeness between me and his father. I had always shared many feasts and close quarters with the scarred male, but I never really felt like he had ever accepted me as one of the family. It opened up a different perspective as he was always watchful whenever his son and I had any kind of interaction. I welcomed the chance for that awkwardness to melt away and for the scarred male to warm up to my presence among the tribe. Big Ears grew so quickly over the next four years that Little Blue and I were able to take him on a couple of hunting excursions and allowed him to participate. He would shine with pride every time we were able to bring home some game to feed the tribe. He insisted on carrying it back to the cave as if he had single handedly brought home the bounty. Big Ears did have exceptional hearing; I truly believe it was due to the size of the ears and his ability to lock in on the sounds. It was something that came in handy and I found myself looking at his reactions to far away sounds. He had a fascination with my clothing and especially my shoes. He was attentive enough to be able to track visually and not only by smell and sound. I would see him studying the ground and recognize the difference between deer, elk and wolf tracks. He also studied the tracks of his family members as well and could stay on his father's tracks in the deepest brush. He was turning into a talented hunter in just a few short years. I was impressed at how quickly they developed into full sized adults; it took about seven to eight years for them to reach full maturity. At going on four years he was over four and a half feet tall and could run every bit as fast as I could.

One day I caught Big Ears fastening some dried skin to his feet with some small pine branches intertwined throughout. I found a flat spot on the rocks; sat back and watched as he tried them out. It was awkward for him in the beginning to walk as I am sure he felt disconnected from the earth. He paid particular attention to the tracks that he left behind and seemed somewhat satisfied with the results. This continued for the next three months as I helped him with a fastening technique between his big toe and the others and strapped around the ankle. He no longer left behind the 'bigfoot' trademark; his tracks were even less obvious than a moccasin track. He had found a way for the tribe to hide some of their movements in the soft dirt and around the streams; something that will come in handy close to civilization. It wasn't long before many of the tribe were using the leather foot covers with the soft pine branches interwoven for a less obvious track. It wasn't just me adapting to them; but they were able to use something from me to keep themselves harder to find.

Baby Girl

It was now the spring of 2005 and the years had been good to the tribe, wildlife remained plentiful over my time with the family. I found myself coming and going into the cave with or without Little Blue; my position here was as common as one of the family. Other than the clothes, hair, speed, strength and stamina; I looked just like one of them. There was a new baby in the cave; born from the male with the red colored hair and his mate. This would be his second child; the first was a boy who had been killed in cold blood by another young male in the tribe years ago. With this new baby in the tribe came plenty of work for everyone as the younger generations were to be the mentors and the adults were to hunt for supplies once the trails were clear enough. It was an adorable fragile looking female; small at birth but hairy, skinny and had big bright eyes with a turned up button nose. She crawled all over everything, and each and every tribe member seemed to have a hand in the upbringing of the children, not just the parents. We were all out in the grassy area below the slide on a warm sunny day. The wind was low and the sun was perfect and many of the tribal members were soaking up the heat. I watched the female and the male with the red hair tending to their little curious girl, but she was focused on me for some reason. She would try to crawl over the female to come towards me but was pulled back by the male who wasn't ready to give her up. This went on for about ten minutes while I sat back, leaning on Little Blue, watching in amusement. Finally the female snatched up the baby and stood up; out of habit the red colored male stood up as well. The female turned and brought the baby girl over and sat her down beside me and Little Blue while the male just watched. This horrified the male as he started to come over to retrieve the little crawler who was already making her way across my lap. One little quick bark from the female stopped him in his tracks and he sat back down with the female settling in beside him. Together they watched the little button nose sweetheart pull at every button and chew on the shirt that I was wearing. It was adorable and fun for Little Blue and me, with the ever so watchful eye of the red haired father staring intensely at our every move. All in all it was a wonderful afternoon, I think the red colored male was able to get past some of his long held grudge against me.

First the vegetation was brought into the cave and then the big game hunting would go into full swing when the cooler months came in. Little Blue and I continued our hunting with the company of the scarred and the red colored male. They had joined us in our hunts over the last few years and were very proficient with the antlers and sheer brute force. I stood in awe as I watched Little Blue actually out maneuver, and take down a young elk running through some thick trees. I wish I had her speed and agility out here in the wilderness. I had been able to keep up pretty well over the years considering my age.

We spent the warm months gathering supplies for the cave and dropped in on the baby female at every opportunity. She was simply an adorable bubbling beauty with energy that kept everyone on the move. The oldest male was now covered in all silver hair and seldom left the cave during the summer months. I had watched him lead this family through the years with authority and respect. He never fought with or had any confrontation with any members of the tribe. It was out of absolute respect and honor that he was never challenged. I had however seen others within the tribe dispute and fight with ferocious and deadly force. Once I had even witnessed two adults take the fight to the death. It was their way of sorting things out. I was thankful that I had never appeared to be a threat to anyone in the tribe as I had no chance against their sheer size and skill. I had become a family member to this tribe, and this would be my first complete winter inside the cave with Little Blue and this new little baby girl. There was plenty of food and continuous water from the stream in the tunnel. I had a new respect for the water in the cave but still needed it to survive. I had taken my longest rope from the cabin and tied it to a stone outcropping close to the stream and secured it on both sides so that I could have my anchor point when passing through the water. It was my own little safety addition to the cave; maybe not for the benefit of anyone else but my own personal lifeline. The sounds in the cave filled with snoring and grumblings of anxious members as the cold months crawled by. There was a new sound of snoring from the little baby girl blowing saliva bubbles while she slept and most of the time she was awake.

It was a cute sound that had me smiling throughout the many hours while waiting for spring. Since she was the new baby, she was the hub of attention from all the other female members. They came out of nowhere, all hours of the night and day to hold her and rock her as she slobbered and snored the winter months away. I would watch her in the arms of the females by the exit opening of the cave as she put her tongue out and blew spit everywhere; it was disgusting and amazing. Spring brought plenty of activities as we finally made it outside into the open by the clearing. After coming out I was anxious to get into the cabin but really found nothing there that I needed. I just headed up to the glacier and cleaned up for a much needed wash. I cannot remember the last time a wash felt as good as it did coming out of the winter cave; the sun was bringing with it the feeling of peacefulness and new growth.

Missing Little Blue

It had been two years since the daughter of the red colored male was born. The little baby girl was about four feet tall and a skinny and knobby knee little bundle of cuteness. She didn't crawl all over anyone anymore, but she would always stand close to everyone, engrossed in what they were doing, as if training to be an adult. She seemed to be everywhere with her big curious eyes and noisy breathing. Her habit of spitting out her tongue and blowing was her way of announcing that if you didn't see her, you would certainly hear that she was right around the corner watching your every move. She was a bit clumsy and had an awkward gate with her long bony legs, but could still run faster than me as a child. She loved the hair on the hides that we brought in; it was expected that she would climb all over the animals that we brought in as she loved the texture of the hair as she combed her fingers through.

Little Blue and I had hunted together for many years and our habits were always understood. If she pursued the running wildlife; I waited enough time to make certain she was not coming right back and went on my way back to the cabin. I was going on sixty two years old but with the physical activity I have been able to feel young enough to keep up with the best of them. There was one I could never keep up with and that was Little Blue; in fact, not any of the tribal members could.

There were four of us on a hunt on the lower side of the mountain range when we got into a fairly large herd of elk. The scarred male ran uphill to cut off the access before they could get past some cliffs and into a thick dense wooded area. The red colored male and Little Blue ran through an opening to the left with Little Blue pulling ahead with every step. The herd shifted and crossed directly in front of them and was actually getting away from the red colored one. Little Blue had enough lead to come close to the lead cow and was not about to slow down in her pursuit. The red male was able to take down a nice sized cow leaving the scarred one empty handed. We waited by the fresh kill for the return of Little Blue; she still had not returned by early evening. The red colored male and the scarred one both grabbed one of the elk and carried the entire thing back to the glacier, I stayed behind at the cave while they went back for the second one. Little Blue was not in the area; something that was not out of the ordinary but she had never really left for this long when all four of us were out hunting.

Early the next morning the two adult males came to my bed in the cave and had me follow them back to the same area that we hunted the previous day. They followed smells and often times would bark and knock on a nearby tree but to no avail. I spent time looking at tracks in the ground to see where the herd had ended up. We stayed on their trail for two solid days before finding them again. Little Blue was nowhere to be found and the two males showed no interest in hunting the herd. It was their behavior that had me concerned; they sensed that she might be in trouble. We continued the search for another full day and set up a sleeping area for the night. This was the fourth night that Little Blue was missing and even with her speed and strength I was getting worried for her. She was my best friend and my constant companion over thirty years; I had to find her. I don't know what I would do if I lost Little Blue. I started to panic at the thought of losing her; it was something I couldn't bear this late in life. She was my compass through life out here in the wild. The search continued tirelessly for the next few weeks and we scoured the entire mountain range.

The two adult males had left their home and families to search for Little Blue. They had a connection with her as only family could, but I couldn't be more grateful and was indebted to these two warriors. We left our camp early in the morning and continued our search for Little Blue; the frustration clearly mounting in the eyes of the two males. It had been three weeks without her and I was starting to doubt that we would find her alive at this point. It was not like her not to return within a day or two as she always had in the past when she would run. The two males took off in separate directions at a ridge-line and gestured for me to cut back into a basin off to the west. I guess it was time to separate and divide in our search; we would cover more ground going in three different directions.

Finding a Prison

The small one room cabin was built behind the base of a tremendous pine tree that spread its roots far and wide across the forest floor. I stumbled upon it entirely by accident and felt as though I had better run from the area. Ten feet from the back of the tree was a rock that jutted straight up for about twelve feet and towered overhead and pushed the tree outward as if to push it away from the wall and out into the elements. The location was perfect for remaining invisible as the thick brush around the area prohibited access without making plenty of noise. The opening could only be seen when you were within five feet of the entrance at the base of the tree between the rock and the thick trunk. I had avoided this area over the years and remembered my conversation with one of the men that lived here. I had never gotten close enough to him to even see this secluded cabin.

I circled for just a quick look around; I didn't want to leave without knowing for sure that Little Blue wasn't here. I knocked on a tree about twenty feet away, knowing that if she where around; that she would hear it. The muffled sounds within confirmed that Little Blue was somewhere inside and was a victim of some serious trouble. Without thinking of my own safety, I slipped into the opening and moved immediately to my left; keeping contact with the rough surface of the wall. My plan was to keep my silhouette out of the mouth of the entrance and try to give my eyes time to adjust to the poorly lit interior.

Directly in front of me was Little Blue, laying on her back with her feet tied together and bound to one of the thick exposed roots protruding up from the dirt floor. Her wrists were also tied together and were being held down by one of the men who was kneeling on her hands. The cuts and exposed flesh from her ankles showed that she had fought hard against the restraints and parts of the bones on her wrists were visible and bleeding. She looked thin and fragile with shallow cheeks; her ribs and hip bones showed prominently as she had clearly been abused and deprived of nutrition and water. The second man sat on her chest with his hands wrapped around her throat squeezing tight as Little Blue twisted and turned to escape the intense pressure. Her eyes were bloodshot and frozen with fear and her mouth was wide open, trying to gasp for life sustaining air. Pushing up with her hips and legs, she tried to knock her attacker off balance enough to break free. It was not in her nature to give up, or not to fight until her absolute last breath. The snapshot look into the room was a scene that I will carry deep in the back of my mind as memories that I never want to see again.

The heart wrenching feeling in the pit of my stomach combined with the immediate fury towards the two decadent men was brimming with explosive anger. The sound of my shirt skimming the rough surface wall behind me was loud and both men looked up in my direction with surprise.

Enraged with adrenaline coursing through my body, I kicked a chair away from in front of me and stepped forward, "Get back!" I shouted, "Don't you touch her!"

The two men quickly moved in separate directions as if to separate themselves from the horrible crime they were about to commit. The dimly lit room was heavily cluttered and left very little space to maneuver without the possibility of stumbling; they certainly had the 'home court' advantage.

I was not about to let them off this easy as I reached for the razor sharp knife secured in my waist band. Lunging forward I cut the thin nylon rope that dug into the ankles of Little Blue and with a clean careful swipe sliced through the rope that bound her thin wrists. With an awkward movement to the side I lunged toward the midsection of the larger of the two men and plunged my knife deep under the ribs of the man who was now face to face with me. I felt no regret; hesitation or remorse in this decision tonight as the weapon reached far inside the soft tissue past the protection of the ribcage. This was a necessary job that would not go unfinished as I continued the sideways movement and forced the steel long ways out the side of his torso. I pushed through and beyond with the assurance that this attack had completed its necessary objective. The first man fell, slumped to the floor without enough life to bring out his hands to slow the fall; this would be his last exhale.

With my eyes wide with anger and renewed focus I approached the second man in the dark corner of the room only to be joined by the battered female who had regained her footing and was looking for a little payback. She brushed past, taking the lead with a primal scream; even in her weakened condition Little Blue leapt forward into the outstretched arms of the second man digging her fingers deep into his neck. In a flash she sank her teeth deep into the side of his throat and bared down with all that she had left; wrapping her legs and arms around his body with a fierce grip. The man's eyes were wide with terror as he clawed at her face to push her away and free himself from the imminent punishment. Little Blue was locked onto her captor with several weeks of unspeakable abuse and torment to fuel her anger. The momentum of her weight and attack brought them both down to the hard surface of the floor in a loud thud. With Little Blue on top of his shoulders and attached to his throat the man flailed onto his side reaching for anything he could leverage himself on to ward off his attacker. I stepped forward and sat my weight on his legs and held him into position while Little Blue forced her teeth deeper into the airway of her enemy.

The violent shaking from Little Blue, the panic stricken thrashing of the second man slowed down and the hoarse gasps eventually ceased, leaving a heavy silence in the dark humid cabin. Little Blue calmly withdrew her grip from the neck of her victim and turned her weary face towards me; trembling uncontrollably. Her hollow features and blood soaked mouth were frightening and gruesome but seemed to carry much less of an impact than the emotion and tears streaming from her eyes. Winded and exhausted she rose to her feet and quietly moved to the entrance of the cabin and stopped; she was finally free to leave this prison and find her way back home where she belonged. Gingerly stepping out into the open air she turned back towards me extending her hands for support as her knees were losing the strength to stand.

Wanting to help I moved quickly to my feet and passed through the doorway; only something caught on the edge of the door that shot pain through my stomach and deep into my spine. Looking down I could see the handle of a hunting knife protruding from the right side of my ribcage, slick and wet with my blood. Over the last few minutes, I had no idea that I had been stabbed with all the adrenaline pulsing through my veins; but the facts were that I had a serious problem through my midsection. My face and hesitation gave me away as Little Blue looked at my bloodstained shirt and the knife handle sticking out of my side and her look changed from exhaustion to terror as I made my way out into the open air. The most noticeable feeling was the scraping of a sharp edge on my rib as my left leg swung forward to step out through the doorway.

My mind was racing as I had to make a choice to withdraw the blade and wondered what kind of hole I would be leaving behind. This was one of those decisions that you attempted to second guess everything as if you ever really have a choice. There was no question that it had to be taken out, but I had nothing sanitary to plug the wound with. What kind of damage it had done to my organs was too soon to be revealed. My mind was spinning with scenarios of how deep this blade was to how long I was going to live. This was one of those things that won't go away and the price could be more than I had bargained for. The knife felt heavy under my shirt and the blood was starting to push its way through the cloth and down into the front of my pants. I put my back against the tree and looked over at poor exhausted Little Blue as she trembled from her own weakened condition. What a fine pair we were, beaten, bloody, and sore but certainly not defeated; and if push came to shove, I'm certain we had plenty more fight left in us.

I pulled off my shirt and assessed the front of my ribs and found what looked like a large Bowie with an elk antler handle and from my perspective it looked huge. It was high above my belly coming in about two ribs up from the bottom of the cage on my right side. How could I have missed that big of a weapon coming at my body; must be losing my edge, I thought with a grin. Placing my feet about shoulder width apart I braced with my back against the tree and placed the shirt next to the intrusive blade and put my left hand on the grip of the elk handle. You would think that it would be easy to wrap your head around the fact that the knife just had to come straight out; and simply pull hard. My hands were shaking like crazy and the thought of pulling this giant chunk of metal from my side was almost too much to grasp and I felt a little light headed. I took a deep breath and gave a little weak tug; just praying that it would come out smooth and easy, I knew better as it felt solid against my pathetic attempt. I just couldn't manage to bring myself to pull this thing out as I exhaled without moving an inch. I closed my eyes again and thought about the motion and the angle I had to use to withdraw the blade without slicing more on the way out; I squeezed my eyes closed and tried to shake off the light headed feeling. Suddenly a strong firm hand wrapped around my left hand and jerked outwards, pulling the blade cleanly from my ribs.

"Whoooaaaack." I shouted, as the sweat instantly flooded my neck and back. Shocked I opened my eyes to see Little Blue curiously looking down at the knife that she had just pulled from my body. Nauseous and dizzy, I instinctively pushed the shirt into place over the wound and looked down at the seven to eight inch blade. It was easily two inches wide and had gone deep; the taste of blood was present in the back of my throat, not a very good sign at this point.

Difficult Journey

My largest concern right now was getting back to my cabin where I could rest, clean up and try to put some stitches in this gaping hole in my stomach; if I could make it that far. It took a couple of minutes to get the strength to break away from the tree which gave Little Blue a chance to pull her energy together as well; I would need her just as much as she needed me to get back home. The cabin was at least two days travel time for a healthy person; we were going to be challenged to get back in three. We moved cautiously in the night, sticking to the low country and canyons for easier navigation but the uphill climb was coming and the two of us were completely drained and exhausted with little left. The sun had come up fully when we finally stopped for a couple of hours; I rested against some rocks while Little Blue pulled at edible roots, and picked gingerly at all the berries she could find. Her strength was down and she was malnourished compared to her usual athletic shape. Her hips protruded out and her ribcage was showing through which made her look more like a skeleton than resembling anything alive. Occasionally she would bring me a handful of squished berries to eat but for the most part she devoured everything edible within a three acre space. Finally she came back and lay down against me with her arms and legs wrapped around me as if not allowing me get away. This was one of my favorite things about her; the innocent dependence and comfort of showing affection to me.

"John Stone, mine." She muttered and drifted off into a restless sleep.

We slept through the entire day and I woke in the dark as the cool night air moved the trees back and forth in a ghostly sway. She was already sitting up and awake but had not made an effort to get me up. My ribs were very tender and there was an odd sensation in my stomach when I coughed. It didn't hurt inside my stomach, it just felt like I had something scratchy deep under the skin. The cough brought with it a deep purple and black blood which I knew meant trouble. It was time to get Little Blue home and try to make it back to my cabin so I could make an attempt to dress this wound. Rolling over to get on my feet was a little more difficult than I expected as my midsection was tight and the thought of opening the cut back up was not in my plan. From a kneeling position the action of putting one leg in front and simply standing up was more than I could bare, so I had to 'climb' my way up the rock's rough surface to get up and standing, but it worked.

The ground we covered throughout the night was slow and perilous as the cliffs and trails were steep and jagged. From the valley not too far off; the sounds of several wolves filled the air and made my skin crawl hoping they didn't catch the scent of our trail or the blood that would occasionally drip from my shirt. The thought of having to fight off any wolves in our weakened condition would be a death sentence for sure. We pressed on for several more hours with my strength getting weaker and hers seemed to grow stronger. Several times it was her strong steady hands that kept me from hitting the ground or falling from the narrow trail over the vast empty drop-offs. I was losing enough blood and strength that it was only a matter of time before I would shut down altogether and food and proper rest would be too late. The familiar surroundings gave me hope as we could see our clearing below the rockslide not more than three miles away. Little Blue sensed my weakness and took on more of my weight as she found renewed energy being this close to her home.

With a shrill scream that echoed across the open span to the ears of her family, she summoned her tribe to come to her aide. I remember hearing an echoed call from the valley below as I slumped to the ground at her feet. I was aware of others showing up and the strong hands of tribe members picking me off the ground. The arms that carried me tonight were those of the scarred male; with the strength I had left, I wrapped my hand around his upper arm and held tight as he powered my weight up the mountain towards my cabin. He had never hesitated over the years to come to my aid and I had never denied him anything I was capable of, this magnificent male and I had a tremendous history; I was lucky to have lived within his tribe. I fought for consciousness as the pain and blood loss took its toll on my body. Through the haze I can still remember Little Blue putting small bits of berries and raw meat into my mouth followed by water.

I woke sometime around mid-day with Little Blue sleeping on the hard ground beside my bed. Judging by the stiffness of my body and surveying the condition of my surroundings I had been here for days.

When I tried to sit up she sprang to her feet and put her hands behind my back and neck to support my weight. I looked down to see a swollen purple wound in my stomach that was scabbing over but looked disgusting and dirty. I had to get that wound clean and take a better assessment to see if there was any chance I could keep infection out. I had been out enough days that I passed through my fever period but was certainly not yet in the clear.

With the help of Little Blue I was able to get to the stream above the cabin and start applying cool water to my wound. The more I washed away the more I didn't like what was being revealed. The flesh around the wound was rotting and the black that showed deep inside was not the sign of a survivor wound. There was no way around it; I knew that I would not make it through this one for very long. Whatever time I had left would have to be well spent and used to finish the final pages of my diary; my life here had been pure and more than I could have ever hoped for. I worked my way back to my cabin with Little Blue holding me steady and came to a pitiful rest back on my sturdy bed. It was time to write; my days, hours and breaths were numbered.

The days that followed were hazy and difficult at best; Little Blue sensed the pending end of my existence and never once left my side. I was able to finish my diary which included my own projected passing and estimated age of about sixty seven years old; but I have no regrets. This was an early age to finish up, and had I not been injured I may have lasted another twenty or even thirty years. Little Blue was attentive to every toss and turn as I tried to rest, she kept food and water close so I could attempt to nourish my deteriorating condition.

On my final night; I knew my end was near as my breathing became labored and the feeling under my ribs was numb and heavy, as if already dead. I was never more at peace and content with myself as the life I had lived was with good family and friends on a civilized front; but my life here was rewarding

and more fulfilling than anything imagin-
able. The family I found here taught me so
much about unity and respect that I knew
that nothing outside these beautiful mountains could have been better. I moved in an
effort to get off my bed and Little Blue was
again right there with her strength to sit
me upright to a sitting position. The heavy
weight of my torso gave me no support as I
tried to rise to my feet and pull at the door
frame to get outside in the cool clean mountain air. Pausing at the entrance I sucked in
several lungs of the sweet outdoors and pushed
myself through the door, outside against the
cabin wall. It made me smile as I recalled the
first physical encounter with one of my most
trusted tribe members and left him proudly
scarred forever. Little Blue helped me make
my way below the cabin to some of the large
rocks close to the slide where I could sit until
morning and hope to see the sun rise. I knew
the end was here and I wanted to face the sun
one last time. As I tried to sit down Little
Blue came up behind me and wrapped her
arms around my chest and sat down with

me, holding me close to her while I felt her heart beat. Holding me close she was firm, yet gentle with a stabilizing affect so I could rest comfortably through my final hours.

"John Stone." she would say in her low tones from time to time.

"Little Blue." I would whisper as loudly as I could manage.

There was no doubt that she heard my voice as she would always give a soft shrug of her arms as if to reassure me that she was there. It made me smile once again to know that she was near and that she would be with me in my final moments.

The horizon began to give shape to the mountains as the sun gave a preliminary arrival notice. As the lines of the contours became more defined the amber colors blended with a yellow hue allowing for the majestic backdrop to contrast with the ranges I had called home for the last thirty plus years. I had always taken the time to appreciate the natural beauty that surrounded me on a daily basis but today held a greater difference than I had ever encountered. Very few clouds were in the changing sky as the sun threatened to come into full view with its glorious display of colors that seemed brighter than I had ever witnessed. I had made it to the sunrise; beautifully displayed for my final hour.

Reaching inside my shirt I took out my diary and pulled her arm away from my chest and placed it in her hand. I only wished that whatever followed this day could be written on the pages of this diary as I felt that this day might be tough on Little Blue.

"Little Blue, I love you." I said as I patted the back of her hand and tightened her fingers around its tattered pages.

Clenching the diary she once again wrapped her arm in place around my chest and shrugged lightly and said, "John Stone, mine."

With the familiar sound of Little Blues voice in his ears, John Stone smiled in the morning light as he gently took in his final breath.

With Honors

The morning was cold as the members of the tribe gathered around Little Blue who was outside by the entrance of the cave. She was in the seated position with her back against the rocks with John Stone's lifeless body against her chest, also in a seated position with his back to her. She was holding him close with both arms as if trying to hold the memories and cherish every last moment with him. The emotion that she displayed was very much human like as she rocked slightly from side to side vocally mourning with each expanding breath. There were tears that ran down her face and soaked her cheeks dropping on to her chest. She had her eyes closed tightly as if to escape the truth of her loss but the words that whispered from her lips were clear enough, "John Stone."

Her little curly haired female companion sat quietly beside her with her head resting on her arm as if to share the grief and help take some of the pain away. Her little hands wrapped tightly around Little Blue's waist as she too became part of the sad procession. There were no sounds from the others as they came out in single file and gathered around their distraught family member. Finally, the oldest member came out into the light with his silver hair moving slightly in the breeze. The decision had never been a question as to whether John Stone was a family member or not, and the honors of this member would be carried out with their culture of respect and tradition. Taking his position on the stone platform he looked out over the tribe and with a nod, initiated the commencement of the services. One by one the tribe began the labor intensive removal of the stones from the slide and the opening grew. The greatest honor this family could give was to bury their dead in this sacred place beside their home, forever united with the tribe. This was something John Stone would have been grateful for and honored to have been respected with such prestige. The tribe continued in silence as the silvered haired male watched and the blue eyed female embraced the lifeless remains of John Stone. Finally the depth had been reached and the previous generations of deceased family members were visible in the bottom of the slide. Every member was a part of this funeral to show their affection and respect for the memory of John Stone. The tribe lined up at the edges of the opening and all waited in respectful silence.

Two males, one with a large scar and one with a red tint to his hair stepped forward to carry the body of the deceased to his final resting place. They stopped at the outer most open spot and waited for everyone to walk by and touch for the last time the body of Lt. John Stone. Taking him into the opening they laid him down gently beside the many that had passed before him, stepping back with honor to allow Little Blue to say her last farewell.

Dropping to her knees she wrapped her arms around her closest companion, friend and family member and sobbed for a brief moment. Gingerly she pulled his over shirt off and held it close to her chest stepping back for a short final pause and looked down at John Stone for the last time. Looking out at her family she looked skywards and sung out her haunting cry, proclaiming her pain. It was a long heartbreaking call of agony, love and loss that echoed through the distant valleys below. As she finished, her younger female companion scurried to her side and held her hand with both her hands as they left the rock-slide together. They stood together with the silver haired male as all the stones were placed back into the slide and the funeral now completed. The removal and replacement of the slide had taken the entire day and well into the evening. The family filed back into the cave leaving only the two females standing in the evening air as the silver haired male was the last to enter back into the cave. Little Blue looked down at her little curly haired friend and gestured for her to go back into the cave with the others. After a brief hesitation she finally understood that Little Blue wanted to be left alone for a while outside the confines of the cave. With her head down her little friend made her sad approach to the entrance and disappeared from view leaving her completely alone beside the slide.

After half an hour of sitting looking out over the rock-slide Little Blue walked up the hill towards the cabin that once was the home of John Stone. In the dark she could see the outline of the cabin and made her way to the front entrance and stepped into the structure. The inside of the cabin was full with smells of her lost companion and the feeling of sadness was overwhelming as she found the small wooden bed structure and sat down on it for the first time. As the tears streamed down her face and the memories flooded her mind she leaned over and laid down in the fetal position and quietly cried herself into an exhausted slumber.

Two hours later a full grown male with a crimson scar came to the doorway and saw the exhausted female sleeping on the crude wooden bed made by the human that they had just spent the day laying to rest. He had waited inside the cave for long enough and came outside to check on her only to see that she was gone from the slide area. His suspicions were correct as he felt some satisfaction knowing where she would have gone to rest. He stood in the doorway for a few minutes watching her sleep and stepped back out into the night to watch over her from the base of a tree not too far away. He would not leave this spot until she is back in the cave with her family and protected by the great stone walls of the mountain.

New Beginning in the Fall

The next six months were difficult on the tribe as Little Blue fell into a dangerous depression and lay on the floor of the cave as if she was waiting to die herself. The loss of John Stone had left her empty and drained of the desire to move or eat. Other members of the tribe just took it on themselves to bring water, meat and vegetation to feed her as she laid on the hard surface. Not a single day went by where someone didn't bring food and tend to her, sit with her and bring fresh boughs from the trees for her to find comfort on the floor.

Even in her weakened condition and lack of appetite the young female was showing signs of weight gain. Little Blue was with a child growing inside her. She was conflicted with her situation as she didn't want food but the life struggling inside her demanded the nutrition to survive. If anything like its mother; this newborn child would be stubborn and fight for every bit of food it could coax out of its tormented mother. The death of the human could cost the tribe the life of Little Blue; and the baby that struggled for nourishment within her. Physically she was inside the cave and lying on the hard surface, but emotionally she had left the tribe and gone to an unreachable darkness that weighed heavily in her chest.

The Scarred will Search...

There was a calm breeze coming in from the west bringing with it smoke from fires far away in the wilderness. A confident adult male made his way to the entrance of the cave and came out into the light with caution as the light change impaired his vision for a brief moment. The bold scar on his face shown bright white as the sun warmed his skin as he smelled the air deeply for anything that might be out of place. The only thing

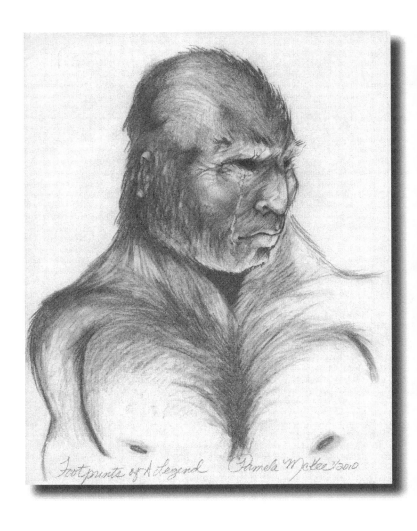

Footprints of A Legend   Pamela McKee 2010

he detected was the lingering heavy sadness from deep within the cave where he now stood. He was not the largest of the tribe but one of the most respected and feared in the territory.

It was time to correct what was missing in the blue eyed female's life. There had to be a way to bring her back into the tribe as she had separated herself with depression and mourning. She would die if they hadn't brought food and water to her, besides she was heavy with an unborn baby and nutrition was vital to the new life stirring inside her.

In his mind he had a plan that was risky, difficult and could possibly upset their way of life, but family was the most important thing in their culture. Another larger male with a deep red tint to his hair came to the entrance of the cave and stood up behind him with a sizeable piece of elk antler in his right hand. He offered the tool to the other who refused it with a heavy sigh and a look of anxiety. As he stepped forward the larger male started to follow but the first male stopped abruptly and held him with a large hand on the front of the shoulder. Nothing could be said or understood more than the larger males desire to accompany his closest friend on this journey; but this was something that had to be done alone. Looking pitiful and rejected the large male took a small step back and watched him leave, making his way down alongside the large clearing. The distance would be far, the terrain would be difficult and the mission could be costly. The male was on the hunt for another mate for his family, but not just any kind of mate; on this journey he would be hunting for a human.

Made in United States
Troutdale, OR
11/21/2023

14790525R00208